I0788713

CRAIG HALLORAN

Dragon Wars: Barbarian Backlash - Book 14

By Craig Halloran

★★★★★

TWO-TEN BOOK PRESS

PO Box 4215, Charleston, WV 25364

ISBN eBook: 978-1-946218-92-6

ISBN Paperback: 979-8-597994-23-9

ISBN Hardback: 978-1-946218-93-3

www.craighalloran.com

Publisher's Note

This book is a work of fiction. Names, characters, places, and incidents either are the product of the author's imagination or are used fictitiously, and any resemblance to actual persons, living or dead, events, or locales is entirely coincidental.

 Created with Vellum

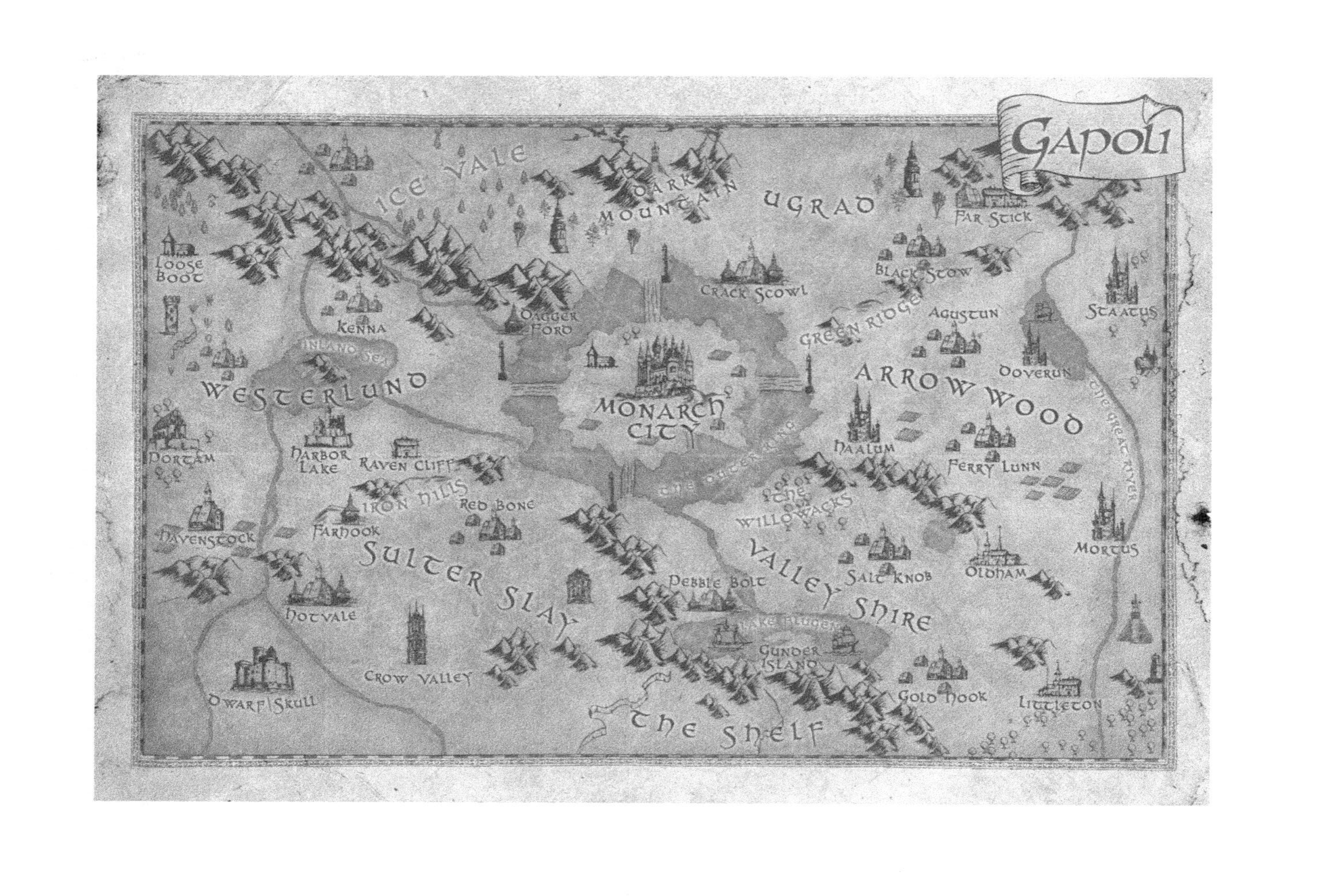

Gapoli
ICE VALE
DARK MOUNTAIN
UGRAD
FAR STICK
LOOSE BOOT
CRACK SCOWL
BLACK STOW
GREEN RIDGE
AGUSTUN
STAATUS
KENNA
DAGGER FORD
DOVERUN
WESTERLUND
INLAND SEA
MONARCH CITY
ARROW WOOD
The Great River
DORTAM
HARBOR LAKE
RAVEN CLIFF
NAALUM
FERRY LUNN
The Other Ring
IRON HILLS
RED BONE
Pit of the
WILLOWACKS
HAVENSTOCK
FARHOOK
SALT KNOB
OLDHAM
MORTUS
SULTER SLAY
DEBBLE BOLT
VALLEY SHIRE
HOTVALE
Lake Flugen
GUNDER ISLAND
DWARF SKULL
CROW VALLEY
GOLD HOOK
LITTLETON
THE SHELF
THE SHELF

THE PAST - ICE VALE TOWNSHIP

"This is the biggest bed I've ever seen." Dyphestive lay sprawled on a huge mattress more than big enough for two full-sized Dyphestives. He stretched his hands and feet toward each corner. "Look at this, Grey Cloak. I can't touch the edges." He sat up and flopped back down.

"Yes, I know. I can see that." Grey Cloak soaked in an ivory claw-foot tub filled with steaming water. He poured a jug of hot water over his head. "Aaaaah! It doesn't get any better than this."

They were lodged inside an expansive suite with pine walls and oak floors. A roaring fire burned inside a huge stone fireplace, and an elk's head hung over the mantel. Streak lay curled in front of the hearth, his eyes closed. The two identical beds, big enough for kings, were layered with heavy blankets and cotton sheets. Every practical amenity could be found, from a kitchen table and cupboards to a bar with plenty of jugs and wine bottles and a stock of dried beef, cheeses, and fruit to eat. A bay window overlooking the township completed the room.

Dyphestive snuggled under his beddings. "I almost feel guilty being this comfortable."

"You might as well enjoy it." Grey Cloak scooped his bathwater into the jug and poured it over his head again. "It won't last."

"I know." Dyphestive closed his eyes with a lazy smile. "But one day, it will always be like this. I swear it."

Grey Cloak shrugged his eyebrows. "Agreed." He sprinkled more bath salts into the water and let his sore muscles soak. As much as he wanted to relax, he couldn't stop his churning thoughts. Lorry, a ferret-faced man representing the Culpepper family, who set the brothers up with the fine lodging, had given him a lot to think about. He'd learned that when they'd entered the Time Mural, they'd gone back in time a decade. It was an opportunity to start over again. And in an odd way, it gave them time—time to figure out how to stop Black Frost. He closed his eyes, submerged himself in the deep tub, and lingered.

Perhaps I can stop Black Frost before he sees us coming. But how far back exactly did we go? The year 6012? That's after we left Rhonna at Havenstock, isn't it? And if we're here from the future, where are our present selves? This is too much to think about, but I have to turn it to my advantage.

Lorry appeared beside the bathtub. His thinning hair was swiped over one side of his head, and he wore the same sea-blue scarf and coat as before. A heavy robe hung in his arms. He set it down by the tub. "How is your bath?"

"Never better." Grey Cloak wiped his eyes.

Lorry handed him a small towel.

"Thanks."

"Anything for the slayers of White Ice. The Culpepper family is eager to meet you," Lorry said silkily. "But they want you to rest while they attend to their affairs. They are very busy people."

"I can imagine." Grey Cloak reached for the robe.

Lorry snatched it up. "Here, let me help you."

"I'd prefer you didn't."

"Certainly." Lorry handed him the robe, turned to face the fire, and wandered toward the mantel. "Your runt dragon seems comfortable. Does he have a name?"

"Streak." Grey Cloak wrapped himself in the robe and stepped out of the tub. "But don't pet him. He bites."

The beady-eyed man eased back. "Oh."

Grey Cloak tied the belt to his robe and wiped his feet on the towels surrounding the base of the tub. "I have to admit, this is a very nice arrangement. I could get used to it."

"We could get used to it!" Dyphestive set his feet on the

floor and eyed Grey Cloak. "That's a nice robe. Can I get one?"

"Yes, of course. Yours is being sewn as we speak. Pardon the delay. You are far bigger than a typical guest." Lorry wrung his hands. "But you will have what you need soon." He moved to the tub and pressed a button on the floor. The tub started to drain. "I'll summon the handmaid to bring fresh water."

Dyphestive smacked his hands together. "Great! I can't remember if I've ever had a hot bath before." He scratched his head. "Have I?"

"I think so." Grey Cloak eased his hands into the pockets of his robe and moved in front of the bay window. The terrace outside overlooked the splendid winter city. It was nighttime, but street lantern posts lit up the well-defined network of streets. "Tell us more about the Culpeppers, Lorry. Do they run the city?"

"In a manner of speaking. They're a very strong family who own much of what you see. Mining is one of their many businesses. White Ice has been a nuisance to them for a very long time. But you vanquished him, or it, rather." Lorry managed a small smile. "The Culpeppers are grateful. I'm excited for you to meet them. It is very rare that anyone gains their favor. They are hard people."

Grey Cloak glanced at his brother. "Is that so?"

The door opened, and a train of attractive young women entered the room. They each carried two pails of hot water on rods that lay across their shoulders. Helping one another out, they efficiently filled the bathtub. Dyphestive wiggled his fingers at them. They giggled and exited the room as quickly as they came.

"If you like, I can have them return and bathe you," Lorry suggested.

"Really?" Dyphestive's cheeks turned rosy. In a goofy manner, he said, "I don't know about that."

"If you decide, someone will be stationed outside your door. Let them know." Lorry started picking up loose clothing scattered on the floor. "I'll have this washed for you."

Grey Cloak retrieved the Cloak of Legends from Lorry's grip. "I'll hang onto this."

Lorry returned a disapproving look. "If you insist, but it won't be any trouble to wash."

"No need." He tossed the cloak on his bed. "So, when will we be meeting the Culpeppers?"

"Soon. But in the meantime, make yourselves at home. And feel free to explore the township. There are many places to drink and eat that I believe you will enjoy. Don't worry about paying. Everything is taken care of." Lorry bowed, slipped outside, and closed the door behind him.

Dyphestive entered the tub and started to soap up. "Look. Bubbles."

"Yes," Grey Cloak said absentmindedly. He took the door outside to the terrace. The icy air kissed his face. He watched Lorry's hasty retreat into the streets as the man vanished into the night.

Streak hopped up on the terrace wall overlooking the township. "I don't know about you, but I think he's shady."

Grey Cloak nodded. "Agreed."

2

IT WAS MORNING, **and Grey Cloak had slept well for the first** time he could remember. He had to hand it to the people of Ice Vale, they knew how to make an elf feel comfortable.

Dyphestive held up his jerkin and asked Lorry, "Are these even the same clothes?"

"The same design." Lorry set a neatly folded stack of clothing on the end of Grey Cloak's bed. "Your old clothing was rotten, to say the least. We sewed new attire for you both. It will be more suitable to wear in front of the Culpeppers. We made more, if you like. I hope you'll find them comfortable."

Grey Cloak picked up a pair of fine leather boots. "This is very nice." He turned them upside down and noted the tread on the sole. "Different from my last pair. Better material."

"Your clothing needs to be durable in the north, as well as warm and supple." Lorry ambled over to the fireplace and fed another log onto the fire. "Only the best treatment for the slayers of White Ice."

Dyphestive patted his stomach. "I'm ready to eat." He flared his nostrils and looked out the bay window. "I can smell something good cooking."

"Yes, the lodge has a galley downstairs. You can go and eat all you want." Lorry hustled to the door and opened it. "I'll meet you down there."

Grey Cloak put on his new brick-colored jerkin, black vest, and trousers. He pulled the boots on over his wool socks then nodded at the door. "Streak."

"Way ahead of you, boss." Streak walked by the door and closed it with one of his twin tails. "That Lorry sure is a friendly guy, but it doesn't go with his voice. Do you know what I mean?"

"I do." Grey Cloak tightened his belt and put on his cloak. "Hop in."

"I get to go?" Streak climbed up Grey Cloak's body and into the hood. "You don't have to tell me twice."

"I'm not going anywhere without you. I don't want any incidents like the last time we were in Loose Boot."

"Lorry means well, if you ask me." Dyphestive pulled a sheepskin vest over his shoulders. "I like him. Besides, shouldn't heroes be treated this way?"

"We'll see. But we aren't here to get a hero's welcome.

We need to move on. Soon. And I'm surprised you're soaking it up the way you are."

Dyphestive palmed a morning muffin from a breakfast basket and put the entire thing in his mouth. "The way I see it, at this point in time, everyone who's dead is alive. It's reason to celebrate."

"We don't know that for sure. There's only one way to confirm it. We have to go home and find out for ourselves. Not everything is always as it seems."

"Who said that?" Dyphestive asked.

"I did." Grey Cloak opened up the door and headed into the hall. He'd stayed in a similar lodge with Anya in Loose Boot. The difference was this place had hundreds of rooms, not dozens. "Come on."

They moved downstairs to the main floor, passing many closed doors as they went. Typical of the lodge he'd been in before, this one had a grand dining hall with a huge buffet of hot, steamy food in the middle. Heads of everything from grizzly bears to elk decorated the walls. Wooden farm tables and long benches would seat hundreds of people, but Grey Cloak and Dyphestive were the only ones present.

Dyphestive made a beeline for the buffet. He grabbed two plates and started shoveling every meat imaginable on them, accompanied by biscuits.

Grey Cloak picked his way through the buffet. He'd become a bigger eater than he used to be, but his plate was half-full. He sat down at the long table across from his brother, who'd begun digging in.

"Don't you find this odd?" Grey Cloak started buttering his biscuit.

Dyphestive picked up a gravy boat among the condiments on the table and emptied it over his biscuits and meat. "What do you mean?"

"We're the only ones eating. Look around. This place is huge, and there isn't another soul around."

Oddly enough, Dyphestive appeared to keep one eye on his food while the other eye scanned the room. "So? Maybe they ate already."

Streak popped his head out of Grey Cloak's hood. "Speaking of eating, how about a biscuit and a burnt hunk of flesh?"

Grey Cloak fed him.

"Thank you." Streak buried himself back in the hood.

"Don't leave a crumb in there. You know how I hate crumbs in my hood."

"Duly noted," Streak replied.

Grey Cloak picked up a knife and fork and started into his sausage and eggs. He sawed a link in half as Lorry approached. The man's hair was parted in the middle this time.

"Hello, Lorry. I barely noticed you in the crowd."

"Ha ha, you are a witty elf. The Culpeppers will like that." Lorry clasped his hands together and stood behind

Dyphestive. "How is your food? Can I have the servants fetch you anything?"

"Do you have any honey?" Dyphestive asked.

A cute servant girl in a white apron rushed from somewhere inside the cupboard, set a jar of honey on the table, and vanished into the kitchen.

With a sausage link on the end of his fork, Grey Cloak said, "That was weird."

Dyphestive craned his neck toward the buffet. "Where'd she go?"

Grey Cloak pushed his plate back. "Lorry, what's going on here? Where are all the people?"

"When the Culpeppers learned you were coming, they vacated this lodge for you."

The blood brothers exchanged concerned glances.

"Why would they do that?" Grey Cloak asked.

"Because you are heroes. You slew White Ice." Lorry smiled and swiped his hair from one side to the other. "And I have good news. The Culpeppers are ready to meet you."

"Great." Grey Cloak dabbed the corners of his mouth with a napkin. "When?"

Lorry replied, "This evening. In the meantime, make yourself comfortable. Our town is your town."

3

____

WITH THEIR BELLIES FULL, the blood brothers spent the day moseying through the township's streets of hard-packed snow. Despite being strangers, the citizens were welcoming, offering smiles, greetings, and polite salutations. Horse-drawn sleds passed by, their sleigh bells jingling. Wood-burning fires blazed in metal urns on every block, where people with frosty breath could warm their hands and feet.

"This is a nice place," Dyphestive commented.

He wiped the snowflakes from his bangs and smiled at a group of young women gathered by an urn who looked his way. He waved. They giggled and whispered to one another.

"It seems normal and pleasant to me."

"Well, don't get too cozy," Grey Cloak replied.

Dyphestive shrugged. "Why not? So long as we're here, we might as well enjoy it. Right?"

"As much as I hate to say it, you should know better."

He nodded at the young women. Much the same as the rest of the township, many humans and several elves milled about. Included among them were dwarves and halflings. He'd even spotted a few orcs and lizardmen.

"Something gnaws inside me. I think we would be wise to depart before we meet the Culpeppers."

"That wouldn't be polite. They just want to thank us. Why would they have any problem with us, when we did them a favor? Perhaps they can help us."

"I see your point, but given our situation, it would be best if we lay low and move on."

Dyphestive taking the situation lightly disturbed Grey Cloak. He had the feeling that something wasn't right with his brother. Dyphestive was too loose, no longer as brooding or loaded with concern. But Grey Cloak kept his concerns about his brother to himself the best he could. Perhaps the time travel did something to him. After all, it altered Streak's size. It might have altered Dyphestive's mind. He decided not to dwell on it.

"We might have more time on our hands, but we can't afford to waste it."

"Ah, I think it will be interesting. Besides, I don't think they'll let us leave without saying goodbye." Dyphestive turned to look over his shoulder and nodded. The township's soldiers trailed behind them at a distance. They were easy to spot, wearing fur caps and heavy wool coats, their swords belted on and spears in hand.

"Yes, I noticed them casually moving among the crowd and following us. I'm surprised that you noticed them too."

"Of course I did. I bet I noticed them before you," Dyphestive said.

"No, you didn't."

"Uh-huh." Dyphestive stopped at a serving cart where two young women, pretty and fair skinned, with ice-blue eyes and blond ponytails, served hot cider. He breathed deeply through his nose. "That smells good."

"Please, indulge yourself." One of the women handed him a wooden mug filled to the brim. "It's courtesy of the Culpeppers. Drink, it gives you strength and refreshes you."

Dyphestive drank. "Mmmmm, that's good. Thank you."

"You're welcome," the twins said in unison. "How about you?" they asked Grey Cloak.

He smirked. "It would be impolite not to." He took the cup he was offered and drank. The hot, spicy cider warmed his insides from head down to toe. "That is good. Thank you, ladies. May I ask you a question?"

They nodded.

"What year is it?"

The twins gave him a funny look, giggled, and brightly said, "It's 6012."

He nodded. "Thank you."

"Come back soon. We'll be here all day, waiting for the big announcement," the twins said.

Grey Cloak gave them a funny look as he walked away. "What do you suppose they're talking about?"

"I don't know, but I'm definitely going to get more cider."

"Here, you can have mine."

"You don't like it?"

"I do, but I'm not thirsty."

As they passed from one intersection of log-built structures to another, something caught Grey Cloak's eye. He caught Dyphestive by the elbow and tugged him down the street to his right.

"What gives? Did you smell something good? More cider?"

"No."

He towed his brother along and came to a stop in front of a building with a bright-red door. The sign hanging by chains above the door read Batram's Bartery and Arcania.

In a hushed voice, Grey Cloak said, "It can't be."

Dyphestive scratched his head. "Should we go in?"

In the past, there had been times Batram had swept them into the store.

Grey Cloak didn't get a sense that was going to happen this time though. He eased onto the first step. "Perhaps it's an opportune time to pay our old friend a visit?"

"Do you think that's wise?"

Grey Cloak took the stairs up to the porch and knocked on the red door. "I'll take my chances."

The wooden stairs groaned beneath his feet as Dyphestive joined his brother.

"That's odd. No answer," Grey Cloak said. He knocked again, harder than the last time.

No answer.

A strong, icy wind swept down the street. Not a soul was in sight, from one end of the road to another. The air whistled through the building's cracks and crevices. The hanging sign rattled on its chains, and the snow dusted up.

Dyphestive gave his brother a doubtful look. "Let me try." He hammered on the door with his big fist. "That door's as solid as stone."

Grey Cloak nodded. "I know. It won't budge, not even a crack."

"What do we do?"

He shrugged. "I guess we go back to the lodge."

4

BACK AT THE LODGE, Grey Cloak and Dyphestive lay in their separate beds, looking up at the rafters in the vaulted ceiling. Grey Cloak flipped a dagger up into one of the wooden beams. It stuck for a moment then fell free, point turning downward, and he caught it by the handle. He did the same routine several times. Finally, he sat up on the edge of the bed and put the dagger away.

"It really bothers me that Batram didn't answer the door," he said.

"Maybe he doesn't know us yet."

"I don't see how. It was 6010 when we left Havenstock. I met him the same year. He would have to know me."

Dyphestive stretched his arms out. "Maybe something else has changed. Maybe he never met you the first time the way that you thought."

"Oh, don't say that. It's hard enough dealing with our current situation." He got up, strolled over to the fireplace, leaned on the mantel, and stared at the flames.

Streak had curled up on the hearth, eyes closed. "Don't overthink it."

"It's hard not to. And you might be in a time where you haven't been born yet."

"Hmmm, that could be dangerous," Streak said.

Grey Cloak rebuilt a timeline in his mind. As he understood it, they were in a time close to when Black Frost wiped out the Sky Riders at Gunder Island. He believed it was after that, but he wasn't certain. If it was before, he could go back and warn them, but he was fairly certain that happened in 6011.

Someone knocked at the door, and Lorry entered the room. "Greetings. Are you ready for your audience with the Culpeppers?"

The brothers exchanged uncertain looks.

Dyphestive rolled out of the bed and headed for the door. He towered over Lorry, making the slight man look like no more than a child. "Will we be eating?"

"I assure you, all your needs will be met. Everything you can imagine and then some." Lorry hurried outside and held the door open. "Come."

"What about Streak?" Grey Cloak asked.

"Your dragon is most welcome."

Grey Cloak picked up Streak and fed him into his hood. "Good."

Lorry led them out of the lodge and into the streets, heading northwest toward the top corner of Ice Vale. A huge, castle-like home made out of thousands of logs stood with its back guarded by the mountains. It had numerous pitched roofs covered in snow, with icicles hanging from the edges. A moat of bubbling mud surrounded the castle-home, and a drawbridge had been lowered. Soldiers bundled in furs and carrying glinting weapons watched their approach from their guard towers.

"So, this is where the Culpeppers reside. Very humongous. It must be a large family," Grey Cloak commented.

"The Culpepper's lineage goes back centuries. They're born and bred in the north. A stalwart family," Lorry said.

He led them into the main entrance. The floors were solid rock, and the walls were stacked stone. Torches hung on the walls every few feet, and the heads of wild beasts and tapestries hung in the grand hallway. "This is the Culpepper Homestead. Yes, it's as large as a castle, but they strive to make it feel more like a home. Come, the audience chamber isn't far. They're eager to meet you."

Grey Cloak heard the drawbridge rising behind him and looked back. They were sealed inside. "I guess they aren't expecting any more company."

"Tonight, they're giving you their undivided attention." Lorry led them through the oversized hallways and stopped at a pair of wooden double doors, each with long bronze handles. "This is the audience chamber. They do not consider themselves royalty, so there is no need to kneel or bow. I only mention this because they can be imposing, but I'm sure the likes of you aren't as easily intimidated as others tend to be. Are you ready?"

"After you," Grey Cloak said.

"I won't be joining you. This is as far as I go." Lorry pushed the doors open. "You may enter."

The brothers crossed the threshold. Lorry closed them inside.

Oddly enough, Grey Cloak found himself missing the ferret-like little man. He raised his shoulders and wandered deeper into the audience chamber with his brother. The floor was made of black granite, and the stone walls were whitewashed. Aside from them, nothing occupied the room but the flickering flames of urns on the floor along the walls. They offered little illumination to the center of the room, which was the dimmest spot of all. They walked toward the center.

Someone spoke in a strong, resonant voice. "Yes, come closer, slayers. We are eager to meet you."

The brothers proceeded forward. The darkest spot on the opposite side of the room began to take shape. Two persons sat in a tall stone chair meant for two: a man and a woman. Standing in the shadows behind them were several more people.

"I am Hercullon Culpepper. This is my wife, Sandal." He held her hand in his large mitt when he spoke. Hercullon had a mane of snow-white hair, facial scars, hard eyes, and a jaw as hard as stone. Like Dyphestive, he was broadly built, and his powerful chest and shoulders filled out his black jerkin, which matched the rest of his dark clothing.

Sandal was a honey-blond beauty, shapely in her fur-and-leather garb, with piercing ice-blue eyes that could melt snow. She soaked the blood brothers in with her gaze and gave them a polite nod.

Lorry hadn't lied. The Culpeppers were imposing, but they were hardly extraordinary like he made them out to be. Hercullon had a muscle-bound build and broad face. They were older, and they would stand out in a crowd, like pillars among men, but they weren't an ettin or a dragon either.

Grey Cloak cleared his throat. "I'm Grey Cloak, and this is my brother, Dyphestive. Of course, you know that, but we are glad to meet you." He looked between them. "I think."

Hercullon rubbed his jaw and studied them. He didn't say a word, and an awkward amount of time passed. Finally, he said, "You slew White Ice. I imagine you didn't slay him with conversation."

Dyphestive chuckled. Grey Cloak elbowed him.

Hercullon lifted his hand. "It was a jest."

"Ah, well, it was very funny." Grey Cloak made an uncomfortable chuckle.

Hercullon didn't bat a lash. He quieted. With his cunning eyes still fixed on the brothers, Hercullon whispered in Sandal's ear. Retaining her polite smile, she nodded.

It was the most awkward meeting Grey Cloak had ever attended. It was worse than the days when he'd been scolded by Rhonna, back at Havenstock, for not doing his chores. Sometimes she would make him sit in a room with her in stone-cold silence. Somehow this was worse. It was weird.

Dyphestive rose onto his toes. "Are we going to eat?"

Hercullon slapped the arm of his stone chair. "Hah! A man after my own heart!" His loud voice echoed through the chamber. "Yes! Now that we've met, we will feast." He let go of his wife's hand and leaned forward. "But first, I want you to tell me the story of how you killed the beast."

"By the looks of you, I'm surprised you didn't kill White Ice yourself," Grey Cloak said.

Hercullon stretched out his massive arm and pointed his sausage-sized finger in Grey Cloak's face. "No doubt I could have, but there's a reason I did not and you did."

5

Hercullon and Sandal soaked up every word of Dyphestive's version of slaying White Ice. Both of them were on the edge of their seats, wide-eyed and almost drooling.

When Dyphestive ended the story, Hercullon broke into applause. "A gritty tale. One of the best I've ever heard. You are brave men, bold men. Men such as you are in short supply."

Sandal hung on her husband's arm. "Agreed, my love."

"Servants!" Hercullon clapped twice. "It is time to feast!" He eyed the brothers. "Follow."

A group of bare-chested, strong-backed men appeared from the shadows carrying long poles in their arms. They slid the poles into rings built into the stone chair and lifted it off the ground. They carried Hercullon and Sandal deeper into the chamber and passed into another hall, where a rectangular wooden dining table loaded with silver platters of food waited.

The men set Hercullon and Sandal down. They moved to the opposite ends of the table, Hercullon taking position at the head, and sat down in chairs. Grey Cloak and Dyphestive joined them.

The dining hall was similar to the dining halls in the lodge. An iron chandelier with burning candles hung suspended overhead. Two fireplaces burned in the corners. As the male servants departed, a pair of female servants in modest robes entered, filled their tankards with ale, and hurried away, vanishing through a small portal near the fireplace.

Hercullon stood at the end of the table and raised his tankard. "To the White Ice Slayers. Because of them, Ice Vale is safer, and my gold is too! Ha ha!" He guzzled down his ale and slammed his tankard on the table.

A servant woman hurried back and refilled it. Dyphestive finished his ale and slammed it down. Grey Cloak took a drink of the bitter ale and frowned. Sandal caught his face and smiled.

"Everyone, eat. I'm famished." Hercullon loaded up a plate of meat, potatoes, and rolls, stacking it up to his chin.

Dyphestive did the same, and both men dug in with their forks and knives.

"I like your appetite. It's no wonder you're so big—as big as me." Hercullon leaned over and elbowed Dyphestive.

"It's a good thing to be big and barbaric." He soaked his potatoes in gravy. "We are descendants of barbarians. Our savage brethren still live in the climbs behind us. We conquered Ice Vale centuries ago, but our root has spoiled. We've lost our civilized ways." He looked across the table and winked at his wife. "But not all are complaining."

"Hercullon is the strongest of them all." Sandal swept her hair over her shoulder. "Every five years, a champion from the tribes challenges him. He must defeat them, or war will ensue and Ice Vale's civilization as we know it will be lost."

"Aren't you on the same side?" Grey Cloak asked.

"One would think, but there is always someone who wants the crown for themselves. They feel their way is better," Hercullon said.

Grey Cloak buttered his roll. "So, you are the ruler of Ice Vale."

Hercullon nodded. "But I have a council that governs the affairs of the township. I'm not one for meetings and ceremonies."

"When is the next fight?" Dyphestive asked.

"Soon." Hercullon exchanged a glance with Sandal.

She gave a quick nod.

"I would like you to meet someone. Our child."

"Certainly," Dyphestive said.

Hercullon made an awkward motion with his hand and stood.

A young woman entered the dining hall. She was tall and shapely, wearing a dress made from animal skins. Her beauty resembled that of her mother, and she had strength in her bare limbs like her father. She approached with grace, chin held high, her gorgeous eyes probing the brothers.

Following Hercullon's example, Grey Cloak stood. Dyphestive joined him. Both of their jaws hung open.

"This is my daughter, Dinah. A little goddess, isn't she?" Hercullon side-hugged his daughter. She kissed his cheek, walked to her mother, and kissed hers as well before standing by Dyphestive.

"Oh." Dyphestive pulled a chair out for her and watched her sit. He scooted her in so far that her chest rocked the table. "Sorry."

The men resumed their seats.

"Dinah is our only child. It's not from a lack of trying, but having a pack of children has not been our fortune. Hence, the Culpepper family is dying off."

While he ate, Dyphestive nodded. Dinah smiled and helped him reload his plate.

Blinded by jealousy, Grey Cloak could barely pay attention when Hercullon spoke, but Dyphestive seemed unaware Hercullon even spoke.

"My family needs a strong seed so it can grow. Yes, I could have slain the ettin on my own, but instead, I sent champions to take it down. All of them failed. All of them died. You even saw their bones." Hercullon took a long drink. "The truth is, I'd all but lost hope in men bold enough to take the ettin down. Then you two came along, you and your dragon. It was as if you fell from the heavens and took out White Ice. I knew the moment I heard it that one of you would be the one to become my heir apparent. The one to marry my daughter and make the family line strong again."

Dinah played with Dyphestive's hair while he ate, and he was all grins.

Grey Cloak kicked him underneath the table.

Dyphestive gave him a puzzled look. "What did you do that for?"

"Will you pay attention? Didn't you hear what Hercullon said?"

"No." Dyphestive gave Hercullon an embarrassed look. "I'm sorry. I was, uh, distracted. What were you saying? Something about slaying White Ice yourself?"

"I'll tell you what I said." Hercullon grabbed Dyphestive's forearm and looked him dead in the eye. "I believe you arrived here for a reason. It's fate. You are here to marry my daughter."

Dyphestive's face dropped. Grey Cloak couldn't help but smirk.

Then Sandal reached underneath the table and squeezed his thigh.

6

"Marriage?" Dyphestive blurted out. "I can't marry. I'm too young."

Hercullon hammered his fist on the table. The platters jumped. "You will marry!"

"Easy, my love," Sandal said smoothly, as she pulled her hand away from Grey Cloak's thigh. "The young warrior is just surprised. He needs time to let it sink in."

"It's an honor!" Hercullon stated in his harsh voice. "Men have given their lives to wed our precious daughter. And this warrior makes excuses? What's the matter with you, boy? The world will be at your feet. You can rule Ice Vale with me." He thumped his chest.

Dyphestive swallowed the lump in his throat as Dinah playfully hugged his arm. She smelled fantastic and looked fantastic as well. No man in his right mind would resist her.

His tongue thickened in his mouth. He glanced desperately at Grey Cloak.

His brother appeared uncomfortable and seemed to be wrestling with something under the table.

Dyphestive cleared his throat. "I feel honored, Hercullon. But I'm not ready for marriage. I have other, er, obligations."

Hercullon narrowed his eyes and grumbled. "Only a fool would tell me no."

"I'm not trying to insult you or Sandal or Dinah." He gave the daughter a long look. "Uh, she's as captivating as the sun, but I don't think I'm ready to be a husband or help rule a kingdom, of any sort."

"You need to think more before you speak." Hercullon leaned back in his chair and drummed his fingers on the table. "Any other man would be dancing on the table and kissing my ring. But not you. Offered the world and he turns his cheek." He tossed his head back. "Ha!" He erupted in gusty laughter. "Ha ha hahahaha!"

The blood brothers shared a shrug.

Dyphestive caught a playful smile on Sandal and Dinah's faces. He regained his wits. "This was a test, wasn't it?"

Hercullon caught his breath, took a long drink, and held up a finger. He set the tankard down and wiped his eyes. "Your faces turned as pale as linen sheets. I didn't know if you wanted to run or hide." He reached over and slapped Dyphestive on the shoulder. "You are truly a good young lad. As I said, any other man would have jumped at the opportunity, but you didn't."

"So, you don't want me to marry Dinah?"

Hercullon shrugged. "I like you, and my daughter does need to wed. Let us consider this to be the beginning of a beautiful courtship." He lifted an eyebrow. "Perhaps you will come around after a long stay."

The blood brothers were shown to ample, cozy new quarters inside the Culpepper Homestead. Dyphestive paced the room, with his fingers locked behind his head, while Grey Cloak made himself comfortable on the bed.

"You've really done it this time." Grey Cloak smirked. "You're going to be the new leader of Ice Vale, a frozen land that offers abundant snow and warm cider." He flopped back in the bed. "Sheesh."

"What am I supposed to do?" Dyphestive tossed a log in the fireplace and placed his hands on the hearth. "I told them I didn't want to marry."

"Yes, you did a fine job. You were so convincing, they gave us permanent room and board."

Dyphestive had said everything he could think of to try to persuade the Culpeppers that he wasn't the right man for the family. He'd spent the rest of the meal trying to convince them of it, but the Culpeppers wouldn't take no for an answer. They made it perfectly clear that they thought he and Dinah were a perfect match, and Dinah made herself more than tempting. "What am I supposed to do?"

"The question is: What are we supposed to do?" Grey Cloak sat straight up. "Did you see Sandal's sticky fingers? Her paws were all over me. If Hercullon saw her, he'd kill me."

"No doubt he would. You need to keep your hands to yourself. It's embarrassing."

"Me? I was fighting her off. The more she drank, the more demanding she became." Grey Cloak shook his head and flopped back onto the bed. "This isn't good. I told you we should leave, but you wanted to be polite. Now look at what you got us into."

"I know. But even you couldn't have imagined this would happen."

"I agree." Streak lay at the foot of the bed. "Personally, I think you should marry her. After all, you could do a lot worse. She is gorgeous."

"True enough," Grey Cloak said. "But we're still on the run. Lest we forget, Black Frost is still out there looking for us. The last thing we need to do is appear in a wedding."

"Anvils!" Dyphestive hit the wooden mantel, knocking it down to the floor. "I didn't even think about that. They're chasing us—or a younger us—across Gapoli right now."

Someone knocked at the door and entered. It was Lorry, escorted by two brute guards wearing loincloths and furs. They carried the Iron Sword and Rod of Weapons, along with the packs the brothers were given by the dwarf Hannibull. The guards quickly departed, and Lorry closed the door behind them.

"Your gear. I thought you would feel more secure with it in your possession." Lorry slunk into the room and sat down on the second bed. "Your meeting with the Culpeppers went well. If it didn't, you'd be swimming in the moat right now."

"Isn't that refreshing?" Dyphestive asked. "You knew about this, didn't you Lorry? You could have warned us."

"And lost my head? No, I work for the Culpeppers, not you." The sly man crossed his legs and politely placed his hands on his knee. "You should be glad. Both of you. You have acted with honor, and the Culpeppers approve of your character. That's a rare thing these days."

"So, is this the announcement going through the township? Are they telling the people that Dinah is going to be married?" Dyphestive asked.

"The announcement was made that she has found a worthy man and a formidable champion," Lorry said.

Dyphestive's back straightened. "Champion? What do you mean by champion?"

7

"THE CULPEPPERS ARE VERY PERSISTENT." Lorry smoothed his slick black hair over. "You have proven to be a worthy son, a worthy heir. You are strong and formidable. You will be the new champion and battle in the barbarian contest."

"He spoke seriously." Grey Cloak laughed. "I thought that was a jest."

"No, it's a prestigious event." Lorry produced a nail file and began working on his fingernails. "Hercullon has battled for the township for decades. He has singlehand-edly kept the peace. Five years ago, he nearly lost his life in a close contest. He isn't as strong or fast as he used to be, and the Wolves in the Rocks produce another champion every year, someone younger and stronger. They say their new champion is invincible. This year, they are chomping at the bit."

Dyphestive looked Lorry dead in the eye. "What happened to the warriors Hercullon battled before?"

Lorry gave a puzzled look. "He killed them. The battle is to the death."

"So, there's more to it than meets the eye." Dyphestive rubbed his jaw. "Why didn't he ask?"

"Hercullon is no coward. He will fight if need be, but the future of Ice Vale is at stake." Lorry blew the dust off his nails. "The contest is renowned in the north. Nobles and dignitaries come from the lands of Ugrad to watch. Even Riskers from Dark Mountain come out of respect."

"Dark Mountain?" Grey Cloak asked.

"Riskers?" Dyphestive asked.

"Don't be uneasy. The Culpepper family is in good standing with the forces of Dark Mountain. We are one of their top suppliers of steel." Lorry stashed his nail file and rose. "I realize you have much to consider. I'll bid you farewell." Then he exited the room.

Grey Cloak shook his head. "It's getting worse. I should have known it would get worse. Brother, we need to leave, and I mean now."

Dyphestive approached the bay window and took in the full view of the peaceful city. He leaned his arms on the window frame. "I'd never have thought a place such as this would feed the slaughter caused by Black Frost."

"Perhaps Hercullon isn't the noble barbarian he pretends to be," Grey Cloak said.

"I don't know. Maybe he doesn't know what Black Frost does."

"Oh, he does. He turns a blind eye to it. Most businessmen do." Grey Cloak started stuffing his feet into his boots. He picked up the Rod of Weapons and stood by the window with his brother. "We have to go. Now."

"You know we won't be able to stroll out of here unnoticed. Perhaps we can convince them to let us leave. That would be safest."

Grey Cloak shrugged. "Nothing is safe, and we can't stand around and hope Black Frost's minions don't spot us. If they see us, we'll be doomed."

"Black Frost has thousands of minions. Chances are, whoever he sends won't know anything about us."

"What are you saying? You want us to ride this out? We can't risk it. We need to find a way out now."

Dyphestive nodded. He put his hand on his brother's shoulder. "I'll talk to Hercullon. In the meantime, you see what you can do."

"Certainly." Grey Cloak moved back to the bed and sat down. "I'll think of something."

"You'll find Hercullon in the training arena. Follow me," Lorry told Dyphestive, who'd bumped into the ferret-faced man as soon as he'd exited his room. "Hercullon spends a

great deal of time preparing for the battle. He is truly dedi-
cated. He carries the world on his shoulders and cares a
great deal about the township."

"I see," Dyphestive replied.

As they navigated the hallways, they passed many
strapping guards with bare chests and loincloths. "Pardon
me for saying, but you don't fit in with the other
barbarians."

"No, that much is certain. But barbarian blood does run
through my veins. I'm what they call a runt, like your
dragon. My limbs are no stronger than a young woman's,
weaker perhaps, but I've managed to make myself useful."

Lorry led Dyphestive down the steps to a lower level.
They entered a vast rectangular training room. Racks of
weapons lined the walls. Marked wooden targets stood at
the ready for arrows and spears. Fiery urns spaced along
the walls and in the corners gave the stone room a warm
glow. Hercullon stood near the middle of the bloodstained
floor.

"I'll leave you two alone." Lorry bowed and departed.

Hercullon worked a weighted club, too big for a normal
soldier to handle. He spun it around his body like a jo
stick. He was naked from the waist up, and the aging
barbarian's bulging biceps glistened. Sweat dripped from
his brow, and the scars that decorated his body stood out
red against his skin. He flipped the club over his shoulder
and unleashed a roundhouse swing. His heel slipped on

his own sweat. He twisted his knee and went down on his hip. "Aaaargh!"

Dyphestive hurried over and offered his hand.

Hercullon waved him away. "I don't need help getting to my feet. It's staying on them that's a problem." Using the club like a cane, he pushed himself up, put the club on his shoulder, and started to limp away. "As you can see, I have a bum leg. I'm not the barbarian I used to be."

8

Dᴜᴘʜᴇꜱᴛɪᴠᴇ took a seat on a long stone bench beside Hercullon. "What happened?"

"The Wolves in the Rocks bring forth a new champion every year. I swear by my boots each new one is stronger than the last." Hercullon unraveled the strips of cloth covering his calloused hands. He cracked his neck from side to side. "I've always had an edge that saw me through."

Dyphestive caught the older man's penetrating stare. "You're a natural, aren't you?"

"Aye, like you."

Dyphestive nodded. He saw no sense in hiding what he was. Hercullon was a seasoned man, not a fool. Lying to him wouldn't get Dyphestive anywhere. "Your leg didn't heal?"

"Oh, I healed, but that had more to do with the

barbarian in me than anything else. I'm not as extraordinary as others I've crossed. I'm as strong as an ox, and I can sniff out a trap, but I still age. In my last match, the brute nearly twisted my leg off. He drove a stone dagger deep into my knee, to boot."

"There are weapons?"

"Of sorts. The contest takes place in a crude arena. Two barbarians enter, and only one comes out alive. It is our way." A bucket sat on the end of the bench. Hercullon picked it up and drank from it. He handed it to Dyphestive. "Here, drink the melted snow of the mountains. It's always fresh."

Dyphestive found a kindred spirit in the brawny Hercullon. He drank and listened to the elder warrior talk about his people.

"I'm almost embarrassed to say, but I wasn't raised by the barbarians." Hercullon stared deep into a fiery urn. "The people of Ice Vale had been battling for centuries, warring off and on, fighting off barbarian raiders. During one of those skirmishes, I was captured. I was young then and became a Culpepper slave. I never would have thought it, but I found myself agreeing with their civilized ways. I became one of them. I became their champion. I've been that ever since."

"Do you still have family in the Rocks?"

"Aye. We don't speak. I don't blame them. They feel I turned my back on them. Perhaps I did, but the truth is, I did what I did to keep the peace. It was the only way to keep them from killing themselves. Heh. It doesn't sound very barbaric, does it?"

Dyphestive shrugged. "I haven't met any barbarians aside from you." He took another drink. "But I can't fault a man for trying to keep the peace. That's harder than fighting."

"Ha! Agreed, Dyphestive. You are a wise young man." Hercullon gave him a hearty slap on the back. "I have my brethren breathing down my neck on one side and the forces of Dark Mountain on the other. I've had my fair share of sleepless nights."

"Which is worse?"

"What, the barbarians or Dark Mountain? The mountain, of course." Hercullon spit. "It is to my shame that we melt the steel for those filthy dragon riders. That is how we survive. That is how we thrive. But the invisible walls will collapse one day. I can feel it in my bones. I see it in their eyes every time they look at me. One day, they will come to take what is ours. I can only hope we are ready."

"And you think I'd want to take your place." Dyphestive smiled. "Do I look crazy?"

Hercullon tossed his white mane back and let out a gusty laugh. "Tell me more about yourself. How did you come to be here?"

Hercullon had put him on the spot, and he didn't know what to say at first. The situation was complicated.

"Grey Cloak and I have been on our own for a very long time."

"I've known men like you. Adventurers. But you're naturals. Have you had another calling? Many are recruited to the mountain. Alas, the Sky Riders are gone."

"Let's just say we've managed to escape their notice." He zeroed in on Hercullon's last statement. "Did you say the Sky Riders are gone?"

"Aye. Black Frost's brood boasts he swallowed them in flame, one and all, as well as the giants on Gunder Island." Hercullon grumbled, "Or so those rat Riskers say."

Dyphestive's shoulders sagged. His stomach soured. He'd hoped they might be able to warn the Sky Riders, but it appeared they were too late.

"You look wounded, my friend," Hercullon said. "Were you kin to the Sky Riders?"

"I've never been kin to anyone except Grey Cloak, but the news you shared is troubling." He decided to pick Hercullon's thoughts. "You seem sad as well. Did you know any Sky Riders?"

Hercullon nodded. "I did cross them in my travels. I was far younger then, like you. You meet a Sky Rider, you don't forget them or their dragons. The world is worse off without them. But men can't hang their heads and mourn. What we have to do, we have to do for ourselves." He took a deep breath and sighed. "So, will you champion the contest for me?"

"Do I still have to marry your daughter?"

"If you don't win, that won't matter, but the choice would be yours. If you win for me and still do not wish to wed, you will still have bought me five more years to find a suitable heir. At least it would buy me time." Hercullon gave him a serious look. "Dyphestive, I feel it only fair to warn you—the champion on the other side, he's stronger than all the others I faced before him. He's a natural too."

"How do you know?"

"I've seen him. They call him Mad Wolf the Berserker. He has every wolf in the hills chomping at the bit. I don't fault their enthusiasm."

Dyphestive stood. "Don't worry about me."

Hercullon couldn't hide his enthusiasm. "You'll fight, then?"

"I'll do what I must to keep the peace." He started to walk away. "Tell me, do you remember the name of the Sky Rider you met?"

"Aye." Hercullon rose. "Olgstern Stronghair. He was the best."

9

GREY CLOAK WAS JUST ABOUT to leave his quarters when he ran into Sandal Culpepper, who met him outside his door. She wore a fur top that exposed her midriff, a long leather skirt, and fur boots. The older woman pushed him back inside and closed the door.

"Hello, Grey Cloak," Sandal purred seductively. With an enticing look, she pushed him back toward the bed. "I'm glad I found you alone. I wanted to speak with you." She stroked his cheek with a warm, feathery touch. "Handsome elf."

Zooks.

Grey Cloak slipped away from her and moved toward the door. "I was going to take a walk. Why don't you join me?"

She barred the door with her body. "We can't do that. If

the servants saw us together, they would talk. That's why I need to be with you alone. Sight unseen." She seized his wrists in a strong grip then placed his hands on her waist and danced him backward. "Dance with me, Grey Cloak. You can dance, can't you?"

His cheeks flushed. The sway of her hips and sweet perfume captivated his attention. His body began to melt into hers. "There isn't any music," he said in a dry voice.

"We will make our own music." Sandal rested her head on his chest. "You're strong. I can feel it. And you dance well. I know. I've danced all of my life."

"Yes, you're a good dancer. Wonderful." He opted to be polite until he could fully understand what was happening. Sandal's sensual, overbearing behavior caught him off guard. "Er, what did you want to talk about?"

With her cheek on his chest, she closed her eyes. "Pardon?"

"You said you wanted to talk about something?"

"Oh, yes. I'm lonely, Grey Cloak. I need a man like you, a young man, to understand me."

He swallowed. "But you're married."

She sighed. "Have you ever been married, Grey Cloak?"

"Well, no, but I'm very young."

"I know." Sandal squeezed him. "I've been married a long time. It's not the same as when we were young. I have needs. My husband is too old and too busy to meet them.

He spends no time with me. No time at all. I need attention."

It seemed odd that Sandal would be lonely with so many fit warriors guarding the homestead. A woman like her could have any man she wanted. "Sandal, why me? There are plenty of men, not that I condone it."

"Don't judge me. I see these men every day. I feel their eyes upon me. But you, you are different." She looked up into his eyes. "I want you. I will have you." She shoved him onto the bed and tackled him.

"We can't do this," he said desperately to the woman straddling him.

"Don't you find me pretty?"

"Of course, anyone would. But it's wrong," he said.

She pushed his hands down. He slipped her grasp, but she grabbed him again.

"You're quick." He kept pulling his hands away, and she kept snatching them with feline quickness. "Zooks, you're sticky."

Sandal giggled and tightened her legs. "You will do as I want, Grey Cloak, if you're wise."

"If I'm wise, I won't do what you want."

She rolled him on top of her and held his arms tight. "I'll scream. The guards will come. Kiss me, Grey Cloak! Kiss me!"

"No, I won't."

"What in the world is going on?" The door closed

behind Dyphestive. A shocked expression filled his face. "Grey Cloak, what are you doing?"

"It's not what it looks like," Grey Cloak said.

Sandal slapped his face. "Shame on you! Taking advantage of my hospitality! You mongrel!" She kicked him hard and crawled out from underneath him, started to sob, and straightened her clothes. "Wait until Hercullon hears about this." She ran from the room. "Guards! Guards!"

"Brother, what has gotten into you?" Dyphestive closed the door and locked it.

Grey Cloak shook his head and pointed at his chest. "It wasn't me. She attacked me. Tell him, Streak."

From his spot by the fireplace, Streak yawned. "I don't know. I was sleeping."

"Streak!" Grey Cloak warned. "Tell the truth."

The runt dragon stretched his back like a cat and shivered. "It wasn't him. She was all over him from the moment she walked in here."

"This isn't going to go well," Dyphestive said.

"You think?" Grey Cloak slung his cloak over his shoulders and started gathering his gear. "How'd your meeting go with Hercullon? Is he crazy too?"

"No. He met my father, or knew him. I like Hercullon." Dyphestive quickly shared their conversation. "And I told him I'd be his champion."

"Interesting." Grey Cloak shot him a disappointed look. "So, he's not mad, you are." He waved at his dragon. "Come on, Streak. We need to get out of here." He faced his brother. "And so do you."

"There's nowhere to run. They'll be all over us. Don't worry. I'll talk to Hercullon. I'll explain it's a—"

"A what?"

"A misunderstanding."

Guards pounded on the outside of the door, shouting. An axe-head split a board in the wooden door.

Whack!

"I don't think that's going to work." Grey Cloak moved over to the window. "This is the only way out. Come on, we need to make a run for it."

"No, I'll stay. You go. I can slow them down."

"I'm not leaving you," Grey Cloak said.

"Go. You'll figure something out. I can hold them off until then."

It was three stories down, and the bubbling moat waited below. "You wouldn't make it anyway. You'd sink like a stone." Grey Cloak backed away from the window, tucked Streak under his arm, and gathered his legs beneath him. "I'll be back, brother."

"You know where I'll be."

Grey Cloak sprinted toward the window, busted through the glass, and dropped through the sky toward the burbling waters of the moat. The cloak blossomed out, and he fell as gently as a leaf.

"Boss, I don't know about this," Streak said. "If you hit that stuff, you'll sink."

"Or walk on it."

"I have a better idea." Streak spread his wings and started to fly. "Grab my tails, quick."

Grey Cloak latched on. Streak's wings beat feverishly as he towed Grey Cloak away from the murky, bubbling moat. Grey Cloak's feet scraped up the side of the embankment, and the cloak folds gave way to the brisk winds.

"We made it." Grey Cloak twisted around and looked up at his room's busted window. "He better make it as well."

A shout rang out from the top wall of the homestead. An arrow whistled through the wind and buried itself between Grey Cloak's feet. The Homestead Guardians gathered on the wall. They shouted and fired their arrows.

"That's our cue to go." Streak spread his wings. "Try to keep up."

"Don't worry." Grey Cloak took off running after his dragon. "I will."

10

DYPHESTIVE KNOCKED the teeth out of the first man to charge through the door. He hip-tossed the next. A moment later, several guards piled on top of him. They tackled his legs and drove him to the ground. One of them used a small club and beat his skull.

"He has a head like a rock!" the clubber said.

"Hit him harder!" another guard said. "Ooof!"

Dyphestive grinned and let the guards have it. Wrestling in the pile and taking lumps on the head, he had his way with the throng. They were strong, but he was stronger. They wouldn't quit, so he did. It was either that or kill them. He took another shot to the head and relented. He collapsed on the floor and faked unconsciousness.

The stalwart guards groaned. Panting, they climbed to their feet.

"He knocked out half my teeth," one guard said.

"Stronger than a bear, that one," added another.

The Homestead Guardians picked Dyphestive up by his arms and legs. "Goy, he's heavier than a mule. I say we drag him down to the dungeon. My back's already aching."

Dyphestive found himself in familiar territory, sealed inside a damp dungeon cell with half the floor covered in rotting straw. Outside the steel bars sat a bucket of water with a wooden ladle. He didn't see any other imprisoned neighbors. He leaned his broad back against the wall. "Great."

"Quiet!" someone said in a harsh voice. A dungeon guard shuffled over to the cell door and stepped into full view. He was a beefy slob of a man with more belly than chest. He wore the same loincloth and fur garb as the other Homestead Guardians. He smacked a club into his palm and grinned. "Don't make me open this door and throttle you."

"No, never. I'd never cross the likes of you."

The guard kicked the bucket across the aisle into the cells across the way.

"You don't want to be wise with me." The guard turned and walked away.

Under his breath, Dyphestive said, "Whatever you say, bucket slayer."

"What?"

He didn't reply. Eventually, the beefy guard settled into a chair that groaned beneath his weight. Minutes later, the man was snoring like a bear.

"At least I have music to listen to." Dyphestive grabbed the metal bars and gave them a firm tug. The metal creaked, and the edges bracketed in the walls loosened. "Hmm, I might be able to do it."

"Do what?" said a woman in a velvety voice.

Her voice came from the shadows of the cell across from him. A woman lay on a cot in the darkness.

Dyphestive pressed his face against the bars. "Who are you?" he whispered.

"A prisoner, like you," she said.

"No need for sarcasm."

"No need for whispering. The guard won't hear you. Once he's asleep, he doesn't wake easily. Usually he wakes when his belly growls," she said.

"Huh, I have the same problem." He narrowed his eyes, but he still had trouble making out the woman. "It sounds like you've been in here a long time."

"As long as I need to be," she said.

Dyphestive raised a brow. "You make it sound like you want to be here."

"I've been waiting for the right opportunity to present itself. Perhaps I've found one in you." She eased out of the darkness and strolled up to the bars. She was an elf, with long, tangled hair as dark as midnight. Her drab clothing was as gray as a stormy sky. She was fit, her body language as smooth as silk. "I watched them haul you in. My, were they complaining. You must be the one who slew White Ice."

"It sounds like you're very well-informed for a dungeon dweller."

The mature woman smoothed her hair behind her pointed ear. "I have very good hearing. Besides, Big Belly over there talks a lot once you get to know him. He can't keep it closed, even when he's chewing."

Dyphestive smiled. "It is nice to see you can maintain a sense of humor, given your situation."

She smirked. "What makes you think I'm jesting?" She leaned her shoulder against the bars. "Why don't you tell me more about yourself? What did you do to wind up down here?"

"I didn't do anything. My brother did."

She raised her brows. "Ah, the other slayer. And why isn't he here?"

"I covered for him, but he'll be back. Someway, somehow."

"That's refreshing to hear. You sound very sure of him."

"I am." He met her eyes. "Now, why don't you tell me a little about you?"

"I would, but someone is coming." She slunk back into the shadows. "Maybe next time, if there is one."

11

Grey Cloak jogged into the empty streets of the Ice Vale township and entered the back alleys. Streak huddled over his boots with his flat head cocking side to side like a bird.

Grey Cloak took a deep breath. "Well, Streak, do you have any ideas?"

"I can fly away from trouble, but I'm not sure what you can do aside from run." Streak shrugged his wings. "You can't run faster than I can fly, so I'd surmise that the snow soldiers will catch up with you... eventually."

"You're a big help." Grey Cloak peeked down the main roads.

It was the wee hours of the morning, and the citizens had called it hours ago, as the bitter cold and snow-heavy winds could freeze a man's bones.

"At least we have a head start."

Streak nodded. "Yes, but what are we going to do?" His teeth chattered. "Turn into icicles out here?" He set his bright-yellow eyes on Grey Cloak. "I'm freezing."

"Get in my hood. The cloak will warm you," he said.

The Cloak of Legends had many powers, one of which was keeping the wearer warm and dry. As Streak crawled up his leg, Grey Cloak noticed a bird coming from the direction of the Culpepper Homestead. It was a snow pigeon. He remembered what Lorry had said. The winter birds were used to send messages.

"Streak! Hold off." He pointed at the pigeon. "You need to stop that bird! Bring it back to me!"

Streak looked up. "No problem." He spread his wings, dashed down the street, jumped, and took flight. He sped toward the pigeon, opened his jaws, and clamped down on the unsuspecting bird. Feathers fell from Streak's mouth, dropping like snow, as he returned. He landed in front of Grey Cloak and spit the bird out. "They taste better without the feathers. Are we going to cook it?"

Grey Cloak took a knee and removed a small parchment tied to the bird's leg.

"What's that?" Streak asked.

"It's a homing pigeon bearing a message." He unrolled the small parchment. "Ha. This was going straight to the garrison. It's an order to find us and bring us back dead or alive." He rolled the parchment between his thumb and finger. "That seems extreme, not to mention I'm innocent."

"Can I eat the bird now? It's either that or I'm going to start to hibernate."

"Enjoy." Grey Cloak searched his thoughts. He needed to prove his innocence, and it wouldn't be easy with it being his word against Sandal's. "Come on."

Streak gulped down the rest of the snow pigeon. "Where are we going?"

"We need to stay ahead of the Culpeppers. No doubt the Homestead Guardians are not far behind us. It won't be long before the streets are crawling with soldiers coming for our heads." He huffed. "From heroes to goats in less than a day. Who would have thought?"

Streak climbed into the cloak's hood, and Grey Cloak took off running across the snowy streets. Avoiding the light, he didn't stop until he found the street that led to Batram's Bartery and Arcania. He stopped in the very same spot where he'd viewed the red door before, but the arcania had vanished. "Flaming Fences!"

"What are we going to do now, boss?" Streak asked. "The shop's gone."

Grey Cloak sat down on the porch stoop and hung his head. "I don't know. I'm thinking."

The night winds carried the sound of baying hounds and wolves in the distance.

"Well, I suggest you think faster. We're about to have company."

"Zooks." Grey Cloak rose to his feet. "I should have

known they'd have hounds to track us." He took a running start, jumped up, and caught the lip of a porch roof. Using window ledges and shutters for fingerholds and footing, he climbed to the top of the building like a squirrel. Every roof in the township had a steep pitch to keep the snow from building up. He fought his way up the slippery snow and nestled behind a smoking chimney. He sighed. "Anvils."

"Well, look at that. You can see the Homestead from here." Streak flicked his tongue. "Who are those guys carrying all those torches?"

Grey Cloak gave his dragon a disappointed look. "Who do you think it is? The Homestead Guardians."

The winter warriors plowed through the snow on sleds pulled by Clydesdale horses. Racing at the front of the ranks were large, muscular hounds pulling at their taut leashes. A quick count revealed at least fifty stout men coming their way. There would be more once the township soldiers joined the throng.

"What to do, what to do?" he muttered to himself. Instinctively, he patted down his inner cloak pockets and felt for the Figurine of Heroes. The Culpeppers weren't the enemy. The last thing he wanted was to harm any one of them. He would avoid bloodshed if possible, but if cornered, he would do what he had to do to save himself and Streak. "I suppose I could turn myself in."

"Surrender?" Streak asked. "I say you make them earn it."

"Agreed. Hang on." With Streak nestled in his hood, Grey Cloak moved out from behind the chimney, slid down the roof, and landed like a cat on the ground. He ran from porch to porch, peering inside the storefront windows.

"You know, you're leaving fresh footprints everywhere. Are you trying to make it easy?" Streak asked.

Grey Cloak stopped in front of a general store, hurried to the door, and picked the lock. He stole his way inside and closed the door behind him. Searching the shelves, he picked up a can of pepper.

"Ah, I see what you're doing." Streak nodded approvingly. "I saw this in a movie."

12

LORRY STOOD in front of Dyphestive's cell with two Homestead Guardians. He filed his nails, his ear bent toward the cell.

Clutching the bars, Dyphestive continued his plea. "You have to believe me, Lorry. Grey Cloak wouldn't do anything like that. It was her, not him."

"Are you excusing Sandal Culpepper of attacking your brother?" Lorry poked his file through the bars. "That's a serious accusation. If I put it on record, it will only make matters worse. Do you want me to put it on the record?"

"Yes," Dyphestive said.

"I see." Lorry resumed his nail filing. "So, you saw Sandal Culpepper attack your brother."

"Well, no."

"So, you're making a false accusation."

"No, listen to me." He pushed his face into the bars. "Grey Cloak says he didn't do it, and I believe him."

Lorry rolled his eyes at one of the guards. "That's what they all say, don't they? After all, what man would desire Sandal Culpepper? She's so undesirable with her long legs and fathomless beauty. How many men did Hercullon have to kill to win her over?"

The guard standing closest to him shrugged.

"Yes, I lost count myself."

"I know it looks rotten, but it didn't happen as she says. I know my brother," Dyphestive replied. "Please, let me talk to Hercullon. He'll understand. I can explain."

Lorry tucked his file under his sleeve. "Hercullon extended his grace and hospitality to you, and this is how you repay him? He even offered you Dinah's hand in marriage. Then you show him treachery?"

Dyphestive shrugged with his hands. "I didn't do anything, but I stand by my brother. It must be a misunderstanding that can be corrected."

"Sandal Culpepper's word is gold. I don't believe her story is going to change. Someone must pay. That someone will be your brother, and if not your brother, then it will be you." Lorry placed his hands on the bars and offered a sad look. "And the sentence is death."

"Death!"

"Sandal is a high-ranking monarch. An assault on her person is a violation of law. The penalty is death. It's always been that way."

Dyphestive's face dropped. He couldn't believe his ears. No one should die from a misunderstanding. Of course, he didn't know exactly what had happened, but he knew Sandal was lying. She had to be. "You have to let me talk to Hercullon. Please. I can straighten this out."

"Hercullon is very disappointed in you. He had high hopes for your future in his family. Now he has to contend with this and prepare for the contest." Lorry swiped his oily hair to the other side. "I haven't seen him this sad in a long time."

"Contest?" Dyphestive put his back to the wall and sank. "But I was going to champion the contest."

"Well, the fate of Ice Vale is in the hands of Hercullon Culpepper now." Lorry nodded at the guards, and as he departed, he said, "See to it he is adequately fed. After all, if his brother isn't found soon, these might be his last meals." He gave Dyphestive a long last look. "Hopefully your brother won't abandon you."

Dyphestive banged the back of his head against the wall. "Rusty horseshoes!" Rock chips fell into his collar. He clutched his head and tugged at his hair. He'd been trapped before, but for some reason, this situation seemed worse. This time, the freedom of an entire kingdom and the life of a good man were on the line. He needed to stop it, but he didn't know how.

"Well, well, well, well... that conversation had stink all over it." The elven woman in the adjacent cell crawled out of the shadows and sat with her legs curled up by the bars. "Sorry, did I interrupt your sulking?"

"Quiet!" The big-bellied guard strolled over to her cell and whacked the bars with his club. "Don't make me bash your skull in."

She stuck out her tongue.

The guard hit the bars where her fingers were, but she moved them, so he missed. He wiggled the club at her. "Keep it up, and I'll come back with the lash."

"You wouldn't do that to a little elf like me, would you?" She batted her eyelashes at him and spoke like a child. "It would hurt me. I promise I'll be good. I really, really promise."

"Watch your mouth, or I'll bust those lips." The guard acted like he was going to hit the bars again and walked away.

Dyphestive heard a chair dragging across the floor and the sound of the big-bellied dungeon guard sitting down.

The elven woman held up her fingers and lowered them one at a time, silently counting down from ten. A moment after both fists closed, the guard started snoring. "Mauk is a sleeper. That's why the likes of him always draw dungeon duty. It's designed for fat, lazy people, and look around. We're the only prisoners."

Dyphestive gave her a curious look. "Wouldn't they worry about prisoners escaping?"

"Oh, of course, but the good ones are on the other side of the door. You saw them, didn't you?"

"No, I had my eyes closed."

"I see."

"What did you mean when you said my conversation with Lorry had stink all over it?"

"Are you daft? Don't you think the timing of these troubles is, oh, what's the word?" She snapped her fingers. "Convenient!"

He scratched his head.

"Young man, put that big skull of yours to better use. Think about it." She dangled her arms through the crossbars. "I heard you were to be the champion in the contest, right? Everyone knows that Hercullon can no longer win that fight. All of a sudden, he finds a champion, and in a matter of hours, the champion is imprisoned." She flexed her slender fingers. "That's what I call *convenient*."

Dyphestive rubbed his jaw. "But why?"

She flung up her hands. "I don't know. Am I supposed to do all the thinking for you? Can't you think for yourself? Or does your brother do that?"

Dyphestive didn't want to admit that Grey Cloak did do

most of the thinking. In fact, the one thing Dyphestive had decided on was that they meet the Culpeppers. Grey Cloak, he had been adamant that they not. "I do my share of the thinking, thank you."

"Good." She slunk back into the shadows. "Do it."

13

TEARING strips from a shirt he took from the general goods store, Grey Cloak covered them in his scent, then added pepper. He made a new trail in the snow that led to a carriage house where sleds were stored among the horses in the stalls. He stuck a length of clothing in the bed of hay and sprinkled more pepper on it. He did the same in two more barn locations.

"Do you think it'll work?" Streak asked.

"It will confuse them and buy us more time."

The shouting of men and the barking of hungry hounds grew closer.

Grey Cloak eyed an exit in the back of the barn. "Exit stage left." He jogged out of the carriage house with Streak's head poking out beside his. Outside, he waited in the falling snow.

Within minutes, the durable warriors from the Culpepper Homestead entered the carriage house. The hounds bayed, sniffed, and snorted.

He peeked through a crack between the barn slats. Several hounds took the bait. They snorted and sneezed out snot.

"What in the blazes is happening to my hounds?" one of the Homestead Guardians asked. "Bloody bones, there's pepper all over the place!"

Streak's tongue flickered. "Well done. And I thought stuff like that only worked in the movies."

Grey Cloak gave him a funny look, shook his head, and took off.

The streets filled with soldiers, but there were more streets than men. At least fifty guardians and hundreds of Ice Vale soldiers were on the hunt. Their tracks in the snow were everywhere, making it easy for Grey Cloak to hide his own steps. He just needed a good place to hide and think.

A lone Ice Vale soldier passing by an alley caught his attention. The man had his back to Grey Cloak.

Sometimes the best way to hide is in plain sight. Grey Cloak snuck up behind the man, summoned the wizard fire, and gave the soldier a jolt.

The man collapsed in his arms. Grey Cloak set him down.

Streak cocked his head. "What did he do to you?"

The Ice Vale soldiers wore long, heavy coats made from

furs and skins over their armor. They wore fur winter caps that covered their ears as well. Grey Cloak pulled on the coat and jammed the cap onto his head.

"Stylish," Streak said.

"Get down in the hood. It's time to blend in."

"What's going on down there?" called a soldier who stood at the opposite end of the alley. He lowered his spear and approached.

"Zooks," Grey Cloak said under his breath. "Um... I found him here. It looks like he was attacked. Moments ago." He waved the soldier forward. "Hurry."

The soldier rushed down the alley without glancing at Grey Cloak. He took a knee and checked for a pulse on the fallen soldier's neck. "He's alive. What happened?"

"This." Grey Cloak's fingers brightened. He fed the light into the man's shoulder.

"Gah!" The soldier's eyes bulged and glinted with an inner blue spark, then he collapsed.

Grey Cloak blew his fingers. "I'm getting really good at that."

Streak popped his head out. "Yeah, I bet you get a *charge* out of it. Why don't you do it to all of them?"

"I'd probably burn my fingers off, and we don't want that, now do we?" He picked up a spear and moseyed down the alley, regretting that he'd left the Rod of Weapons back at the Homestead. He noticed a squad of soldiers making tracks down the streets and joined the rear rank. No one paid him any mind. They were too busy looking up and down the alleys and roads. He hung with them for at least an hour, weighing his options.

I need to find a way to free Dyphestive. Hmm... he's inside a stronghold, probably being tortured, and oddly enjoying it, while I'm dancing in the snow. Let's see. No allies. No good plans. It's me and Streak against a stronghold of barbarians. Well, amateur barbarians. A crazy woman is in love with me. I can't really fault her, even though something about the situation reeks.

Now, what was it that my brother told me? Ah, yes, he said Hercullon mentioned that Black Frost has already wiped out the Sky Riders. If we only could have prevented that, going back in time would have been worth it. We're ten years back. Where do we even start? Especially when my brother's trapped.

The horse-drawn sleigh ridden by Ice Vale soldiers drove by. It turned down another street and vanished from sight. It reminded Grey Cloak of Crane. The older man was dead, but in the past.

"Crane!" he muttered, drawing a look from a soldier in front of him. Grey Cloak faked a cough and turned his head side to side, as if searching.

He's alive in the past. Most of them are. If anyone can help, he can. All I need to do is find the Brotherhood of Whispers. There's more than one in every town, Crane always said.

Grey Cloak abandoned the squad of soldiers when they turned down the next street. He backtracked and huddled in the shadows of an alley they'd already passed. He moved behind a group of rotten crates and barrels and began rummaging through his pockets. "Oh my."

Streak popped his head out. "Whatchya got there?"

"Potions. It seems Tatiana really loaded me up with potions from the Wizard Watch's Treasure House. Zooks, there must be a dozen of them." He cocked his head. "Eh, what's this?"

Streak flicked out his tongue. "It looks like a scarf to me."

"It's not just any scarf. It's the Scarf of Shadows. That little sneak Zora must have stuck it in my pocket. But why?" Grey Cloak chuckled and smirked. "I don't know why, but I just thought of something."

"Care to share?" Streak asked.

"You'll learn along the way. It's time to break my brother out of jail." He put on the scarf. "And they won't even see us coming."

14

THE HEAVYSET GUARD ambled over to Dyphestive's cell door with a covered platter of food. He held the key ring in one hand and the tray in the other. "Back off. Against the wall, now."

Dyphestive complied.

Using his greasy fingers, the dungeon guard twisted the key inside the lock and swung the door half-open. He shoved in the tray of food and quickly locked the door again. With a snarl on his face, he said, "If it were up to me, I'd let you starve, then I'd kill you. Shove the tray through the bars when you finish."

"Thanks," Dyphestive said politely.

The dungeon guard stepped back into view, knitted his wooly eyebrows, shook his head, and disappeared again, muttering to himself, "Thank you, he says." He let out a throaty laugh.

Dyphestive lifted the cloth napkin off the tray, revealing four pieces of chicken, all which had been gnawed to the bone. Only a few large biscuit crumbs remained on the platter with it. He snorted. "This looks wonderful." He tucked the napkin in his shirt. "I hope I can eat it all."

"Ah-hahahaha!" the dungeon guard laughed. He reappeared, his eyebrow raised. "Oh, I see you have a sense of humor. It won't last." His belly jiggled when he laughed again. "I have a sense of humor too. Mauk has a fine sense of humor." He picked up the water bucket and tossed the water on Dyphestive. "That ought to help you wash it down." He punted the bucket and walked away. "Egg sucker."

Dyphestive dabbed his face with his napkin and tossed it aside. He'd eaten his fill earlier in the day, but his belly began to groan. He looked longingly at the plate. "I love chicken and biscuits."

Sitting cross-legged, he sulked with his chin resting on his fists as he gathered his thoughts. He put a great deal of effort into what the woman in the other cell said. He believed he'd figured it out, in part.

Mauk resumed his routine snoring.

Not long after, Dyphestive heard, "Psst."

The elf woman had moved to the front of her cell and

sat leaning against the bars. She brushed her messy black hair from her eyes. "Are you pouting?"

"No." He sat up straight and lifted his chin, maintaining a determined expression. "I'm thinking."

"Oh, it looks hard for you."

He frowned.

"Don't take it personally," she replied coolly. "But big fellas like you aren't known for thinking. But it looks like you've been trying. Care to share?"

"I'd rather not."

"Why?"

"I don't know you."

"That's a fine thing to say to a person who's been trying to help you. Of course, I have thick skin. You won't hurt my feelings." She turned her back to the bars and started humming and drumming her hands on the floor.

Dyphestive eyed her suspiciously. There was something unique about the elven woman. She reminded him of the first time he and Grey Cloak ran into Than across the Iron Hills near Farhook. But Than had appeared mad, and she was nothing of the sort, aside from nosy. "What's your name?"

She stopped humming and turned around. "My friends would call me Tula, except I don't have any." She stuck her arms and feet through the bars and made herself comfortable. "Now that we've come to know each other, a chip for your thoughts?" She showed a silver coin pinched between her thumb and finger. "Come now, what's the harm in talking to me, a smart, older woman?"

"Who's locked in a dungeon."

"That's the pot calling the kettle black." She smirked and motioned with her hand. "Come on, open up. You know you want to."

He moved closer to the bars and listened for Mauk's snoring. "Fine. I thought a great deal about what you said in regard to convenience. The only person in real danger is Hercullon. He put his trust in me to be his champion, but without a champion, he's doomed. I hate to think it, but Sandal must want him gone. But why?"

Tula shrugged. "Women have their own ambitions."

"I know. I've seen it with my own eyes. They can be serpents in the grass." He looked her in the eyes. "The problem is how do I convince Hercullon? He'll never believe me."

"That's a problem." Tula began flipping the coin with her thumb and easily catching it. "It seems that Sandal's in league with the Wolves in the Rock."

"Or worse. She's in league with Dark Mountain."

Tula's eyes widened. "Interesting. What makes you think that?"

"Because they're behind everything."

15

FULLY INVISIBLE, Grey Cloak made his way to the edge of the township. A long stretch of open, snowy terrain waited between him and the Culpepper Homestead. A small group of Homestead Guardians guarded the road into town that led back to the fortress. The well-built men stood in the stiff wind, half-naked in buckskin clothing and fur boots. If the savage warriors were cold, they showed no sign of it as their dark eyes probed the area in all directions.

With Streak well-concealed in Grey Cloak's hood, Grey Cloak made his move to an empty horse-drawn sleigh. He slipped between two guardians who had their backs to him, climbed into the sled, and grabbed the reins.

The two Clydesdale horses nickered and snorted. They shook the snow from their manes. Grey Cloak tugged the reins. The horses stomped their hooves but didn't budge.

Knowing any sudden action would dispel his invisibility, he urged the horses in a low voice, "Go. Go."

"I don't think that's going to work." Streak started to crawl out of the hood.

"No, stay put, or they'll see you."

A guardian turned and eyeballed the sleigh. He approached with his spear lowered. Grunting, he poked around the sled's floor.

Grey Cloak shuffled his feet out of the way several times, avoiding the jabbing spear. The guardian stared right at him, scratched his fuzzy beard, turned, and walked away.

"That was close," he muttered. "We need to get these horses moving."

"Listen, I have an idea. You have to trust me," Streak said.

Grey Cloak gave in. "Fine."

The moment Streak crawled out of the hood, the runt dragon appeared. He quickly scurried onto one of the horses' backs and latched on. He turned his head back toward Grey Cloak. "Hold on." He sank his claws into the horse's back.

The Clydesdale jumped off its front hooves, came down, and hit the snow running. Both horses bolted in a unified effort and tore through the snow.

The guardians gave chase. One of the burly warriors ran like his legs were on fire and started to close the gap.

"Uh-oh," Grey Cloak muttered. Clydesdales weren't known for speed. Plenty of men could run with them. With the wind in his face, he said, "Streak, we're going to have company. Make them go faster!"

"Easier said than done."

The guardian continued to close the gap. His fingers stretched for the back rail of the sleigh. A hand's span away, the warrior slipped, lost his footing, and tumbled in the snow.

Grey Cloak caught his breath. "Horseshoes, that was close. Streak, we're in the clear."

"Good." The small dragon turned around. "It's strange not being able to see you. So, what's the plan? We could have walked."

"True, but I wanted to arrive in style."

"Cool." Streak started to sing a cheerful ditty. "We're going on a sleigh ride, out on the ridgeline, sleigh ride, woo-hoo!"

They came to a stop at the edge of the moat outside the Culpepper Homestead, and Streak hid in Grey Cloak's hood. The drawbridge lowered, and a squad of Guardians stormed outside. The men searched the sled with confused expressions and stopped when the guardians chasing the sleigh finally caught up. The half barbarians started arguing. A fight broke out among them, their fists hitting muscle and bone.

Grey Cloak made his move, crossed the drawbridge,

and entered the fortress, leaving the fracas drawing more attention far behind. He stole through the stronghold, searching for Dyphestive.

He must be in the dungeon. He crept through the hallways. *If I were a dungeon, where would I be? Near the barracks? Training grounds?* He tailed a pair of guardians patrolling the hallways.

The men talked quietly between themselves about wrapping up the end of their shift. "Hercullon no longer has a champion. He must battle a wolf far younger and stronger. It will be the end of him without a champion."

"Why don't you do it?" the older guardian quipped.

"I like having my head on my shoulders. I've seen this man. He's like no other. Even a young Hercullon would be outmatched," the younger guardian said from his position on the left.

The guardian on the right replied, "You shouldn't speak so of our leader."

"I would die for him. But in the days hence, we'll have a new leader unless someone rises to stop him."

The guardians moved toward the back end of the fortress, where the barracks were located.

The guardian on the left pointed toward a portal that opened before a flight of stairs going down. "And I thought the White Ice Slayer would be our champion. It's a shame he couldn't keep his hands to himself."

Grey Cloak broke away from the guardians and took

the steps leading down. He crinkled his nose. *Yes, this is where the dungeons must be. You can always tell by the stink.*

He flew down the stone staircase that bent toward the right and spiraled downward. It opened up in the main dungeon guard prep room. Wooden lockers, weapons racks, a couple of small tables, and wooden chairs decorated the chamber. Two guardians sat at a table facing one another, playing with a deck of cards. A quick look revealed they were playing a game of birds.

Two ravens and an eagle. A good hand. He moved behind the other guard. *Three doves. A bad hand.* Grey Cloak watched them push coins across the table. *Hah, this fool is going to bluff. Will he fail, or is his colleague a bigger fool?*

The guard with two ravens and an eagle folded. The other flopped his three doves down and grinned.

"Cheater!" shouted the guard who'd lost. He flipped over the table and pulled a knife. "It's impossible that I would lose that many times."

"Put that steel away, or I'll make you eat it," the winning guard said.

"Never!" The loser pounced.

Both men collided and fought for control of the knife.

These brutes are a short-tempered lot. The steel door with a square portal to the main dungeon was sealed shut. A key ring hung on a peg beside it. Grey Cloak opened the door while the guardians were distracted with trying to kill each other. He put the key back, slipped inside, and closed the door behind him.

The main aisle of the dungeon was lined with steel bars enclosing cells made of huge stones. An intersection created a second aisle. A large dungeon guard with a generous midsection leaned back in his chair, his back to the wall and arms crossed, as he snored.

Grey Cloak crept by him. *He's a massive one. Whew. A smelly one too.*

After three more steps, he turned, and found himself looking at his brother, who sat on the floor with a serious look on his face. Grey Cloak smiled. *This ought to be fun.*

16

———

GREY CLOAK FELT eyes on his back and turned. He met the gaze of an older, wild-haired elven woman, and a tingle went down his spine. He moved his head and shoulders side to side. Her eyes followed him.

Can she see me?

Dyphestive climbed back to his feet. He had a metal saucer in his hands and shoved it through the crack between the bars. He let it fall and rattle to a stop on the floor.

After a quick double take between the two prisoners, Grey Cloak noticed the woman's eyes were no longer on him but on Dyphestive. He didn't know what to make of her. If he revealed himself, she could sound the alarm. He took a quick walk through the dungeon and noticed that the other cells were empty. When he returned, he heard Dyphestive and the woman talking quietly.

"Have you figured out what you're going to do?" the elven woman asked.

"I don't know. I could overpower the guards and warn Hercullon. But a lot of men would get hurt along the way," Dyphestive replied.

"What are you going to do, rip the bars apart? They're very thick," she said.

Dyphestive tested the bars. "I could do it. But it would make a lot of noise. I'd have to act quick."

"It sounds like a crude plan. You remind me of an old friend of mine, a strong, bull-headed man who wanted to fight his way through everything." Her stare landed on Grey Cloak. "Perhaps there is a better way."

Did she just look at me? How can she see me?

"You know, you aren't very helpful, Tula. I think Mauk would be better." Dyphestive scratched his head and sat back down. "I have to act now. The contest is soon."

Grey Cloak picked up the metal plate and slowly lifted it off the ground. He tossed it up and down before Dyphestive's widening eyes.

"Are you doing that?" Dyphestive asked Tula. "Are you a witch?"

With her arms crossed, she leaned back on her door. "Neither. I think you have a visitor."

Grey Cloak pulled down the Scarf of Shadows and reappeared.

"Grey!" Dyphestive blurted.

The guard stirred and grumbled.

Grey Cloak pushed his hand through the bars and covered his brother's mouth. "Sssssh." He peeked back at the guard and saw him still sleeping. "No need to alert the entire fortress."

"How'd you get the Scarf of Shadows?" Dyphestive asked.

"Apparently, Zora snuck it into my cloak." He turned and looked at Tula. "Is this a friend of yours?"

"I don't know."

"Tula, is it?" Grey Cloak asked. "Could you see me?"

Tula shrugged. "I have a strong sense of awareness."

"Nice to meet you. Thanks for keeping my brother company, but we have to go now."

"I see," she said. "It's nice to meet you as well. I'm glad to see you have manners."

Grey Cloak squatted down, rubbed his chin, and studied the lock. "I can have you out of here in no time. Getting you out of the Homestead is another matter, but I have a plan."

"No, wait," Dyphestive said. "We have to save Hercullon."

"No, *we* don't."

Streak popped his head out of the hood. "Hello, Dyphestive."

"Hey. Streak." Dyphestive reached through the bars and petted the small dragon. "I need you to help me talk some sense into my brother. We have to help Hercullon. He's being set up. They're going to kill him."

Streak crawled out of the hood and walked over to Tula. She reached through the bars and pet him.

"Hello, pretty lady. I'm Streak."

"I'm Tula." She caressed his earholes with her finger, and he rolled onto his back.

"I love that. Do my belly."

"Streak, leave her alone," Grey Cloak said with a sigh. "Brother, the sooner we leave this place, the better. It's not our problem."

"I'm not leaving." Dyphestive crossed his arms. "We have to convince Hercullon that Sandal set him up. She wants to kill him."

"And you know this how?"

"I don't. It's a guess."

"A guess?" Grey Cloak lifted a brow and looked at Tula. "Did she plant this seed in your mind?"

"No. Well, she got me thinking. Think about it, Grey. Hercullon finds a champion to the contest, and all of a sudden, the champion gets locked up. Hercullon can't win the fight. He has a bad leg. They're setting him up. I know it in my gut."

Grey Cloak leaned his head back and sighed. He'd heard the guardians talking about Hercullon earlier. Even they didn't have faith in their leader winning. What Dyphestive said made sense. "Even if you are right, it'll be difficult to prove it to Hercullon."

Dyphestive pushed his face against the bars. "Find Sandal and Lorry. They have to be behind this."

He nodded. "I'll do it." He picked up Streak and looked at Tula. "Stop planting seeds in my brother's head, please."

Tula smirked. "He did it all on his own. Can your little dragon stay with me? I like his company."

Grey Cloak gave her a doubtful look, shook his head, lifted the scarf over his nose, and disappeared.

17

GREY CLOAK STOLE through the Culpepper Homestead, searching for Hercullon and Sandal's quarters. On cat's feet, he moved up a grand staircase, passing servants along the way. Once he made his way to the top, he moved down the hallway. A long carpet covered the floor, and rooms with closed doors stood behind high archways. Between each door was a bust of a man on a pedestal, with a painting of the conquering hero slaying a beast behind it.

Each large painting stood out on its own—Herculean men carrying great swords and battle axes as they slew terrifying monsters and beasts. Blood dripped from steel. Iron-hard muscles bulged beneath bronzed skin. Where evil once stood, a good man hewed it down. The Culpeppers were men of renown, but it appeared that legacy was about to end.

Two bronze doors underneath a grand archway stood waiting at the end of the hall. A pair of Homestead Guardians stood sentinel. The muscular warriors wore metal headbands and sword belts over loincloth and carried ancient spears.

Grey Cloak passed his hand in front of their eyes. They didn't blink.

This has to be Hercullon's quarters.

He took a knee and pressed his ear to the door. He heard voices inside, more than one, but the door was thick, and he couldn't make out the words, though one voice was deeper than the rest.

I need to get in there.

One of the guardians shifted on his feet.

Grey Cloak noticed the man looking in his direction. He didn't move. He didn't breathe. The guardian turned his gaze away and looked straight back down the hall.

The double doors opened inward. Hercullon stood inside the room, towering over Sandal and Lorry. He wore a wolf-fur cape over his wide shoulders, a loincloth, and fur boots. "The contest has been moved up to tomorrow. I need to train."

Sandal hurried over to him and threw her arms over his shoulders. She wore a silky black robe, and her fingernails and toenails were painted black. "My love, you are so brave and so strong. I know you will be victorious."

Hercullon nodded. "We have no other choice." He

kissed her on the forehead. "No matter what, my love, you will be safe. I promise."

Grey Cloak quickly crawled into the room.

"I'll always stand by you." Sandal stroked the long silvery-blond braids in her hair. "Train well, my love."

Hercullon headed down the hall with a noticeable limp in his step. One of the sentries went with him.

Sandal closed them inside, leaned against the split in the doors, and said to Lorry, "And if all goes to plan, my husband will die tomorrow, and Ice Vale will be ours."

Lorry raked his fingers through his oily hair. "Long live Black Frost."

Grey Cloak's heart skipped. *I knew that man was sleazy.*

Sandal walked right up to Lorry and fully kissed him.

Ew! I really didn't see that coming. I need to wash my eyes.

She moved the smaller man toward the bed and pushed him onto the mattress. She pounced on him the same way she had Grey Cloak.

This seems very familiar and even more awkward. I might gag.

Streak whispered in his ear, "This is the same as the last time."

Sandal stopped kissing Lorry. She sat up with her back rigid. "Did you hear that?"

"The only thing I hear is my heart pounding," Lorry replied.

"Shush!" A dagger appeared in her hand. She climbed off the large bed, narrowed her eyes, and prowled the room. "I swear I heard something." She looked right over Grey Cloak, who was huddled beside a wardrobe. She moved straight toward it.

Zooks. She sees me.

Without warning, Sandal flung open the wardrobe doors. She rummaged through the garments.

"No need to be jumpy," Lorry said, "but I'd be happy to check under the bed. No one's there." He patted the mattress. "Please, come back, while we have a moment to ourselves."

"The moment's passed." She closed the wardrobe and tucked her dagger away in a sheath on her inner thigh.

Grey Cloak did a double take between the two. *Her and him. I don't understand it. Scrawny and gruesome meets savage beauty. They'd probably have gorgeous children.*

Sandal strolled back toward the bed. "With so much at stake, I'm not going to take any chances. We're so close to taking Ice Vale for ourselves."

"After all the planning I've done to make this come together—hah—I'm not about to let it be undone. I've been waiting for this moment all my life. I hate the barbarians." Unmistakable hatred burned in Lorry's gaze. "The dullards have served their purpose. Now the time has come to wipe them out."

"Yes, the Culpepper legacy will be wiped out, and so will the Wolves in the Rocks unless they cooperate." She sat down behind her vanity and began undoing her braids. "I must admit, I'll be sad to see them go. They've been entertaining."

"The entertainment isn't over yet. It will be fun seeing Hercullon getting the blood beat out of him." Lorry slid over the bed, moved in behind her, and helped her undo her braids. "I hate the braids. They aren't you."

She smiled. "I know, but Hercullon likes it." She looked at Lorry through the vanity mirror. "So, what are we going to do about our prisoner? We can't leave the likes of him alive very long."

"Agreed. Don't worry. We'll take care of him once Hercullon is gone." Lorry massaged her shoulders. "Or we'll let him rot in the dungeons. You know, starve him to death. There are so many ways to take a man apart."

Grey Cloak felt his cheeks warm and tamped down the urge to send them to an early grave. *This pair is diabolical.*

"A man like that won't be easy to take down," Sandal said. "Neither will his elven brother. They're special, given they took down White Ice. No ordinary men could do that."

You got that right.

"Oh, I know," Lorry replied. "If we get rid of one, I don't think we'll have to worry about the other. The elf will have to move on. Either that or fight the forces of Dark Mountain. I don't think anyone has the stones to do that."

You got that wrong, you dirty bootlicker.

"Our moment of triumph is near." Lorry leaned down and kissed her cheek. "Nothing can stop us now."

Grey Cloak simmered. *We'll see about that.*

18

"Tell me, Dyphestive, how long have you and your brother been brothers?" Tula asked.

He sat with his back leaning against the bars, listening to Mauk's rhythmic snoring. "All of my life, I suppose. It's hard to say because I can't remember being without him."

"I see." She tapped on the metal bars with her fingernail. "It's obvious that you are different, so I'm curious how you came to be brothers?"

"We made a pact when we were young and became blood brothers. We couldn't trust anyone but each other."

"Interesting. Where were you raised?"

"Why do you care?"

"I'm only making conversation. And why wouldn't I? After all, I'm hoping you'll free me."

He turned his head and gave her a sideways glance.

"Don't get your hopes up. We don't even know what you're in here for. Maybe you killed someone."

"Do I look like a killer?"

"I've known killers far less intimidating than you."

"You find me intimidating?" she asked in her smooth, confident voice.

"Only compared to the others I've known."

"Well, if I'd killed someone, the Culpeppers would have killed me. They're quick to dispense justice. I'd be buried in a frozen hole with my head in my lap. Unless they fed me to the wolves, then I'd be a dung heap... eventually."

He scrunched his nose. "That's an awful way of putting it."

"Everyone returns to the dirt eventually. It's inevitable." She cleared her throat. "But if it makes you more comfortable, I was a servant, and they caught me stealing."

"Great. A thief." He nodded. "What did you steal?"

"Only a few baubles."

"From where?"

"One of Sandal's jewelry boxes." She gave a proud look. "I was cleaning her quarters when she caught me. I couldn't help myself. I have a hungry eye when it comes to jewelry, and she had so much. I didn't think she'd miss a little." She dangled a gold-and-emerald bracelet between the bars. "Isn't it beautiful?"

He couldn't hide his incredulity. "How do you have that?"

"They didn't find everything I took. I'm a pretty good thief. But the guardians shook most of it out of me." She chuckled. "You should have seen Sandal. She was furious. She wanted me killed on the spot, but Hercullon spared me."

"What will happen?"

"They'll hold a trial. Usually in cases such as mine, they cut off the thief's fingers or hands." She spread her long, elegant fingers. "You can't steal what you can't pick up."

Dyphestive turned his back. "Well, you're still a thief, and it's not our business."

"True, true..." Her voice trailed off. She leaned back against the bars. "I take full responsibility for my mistakes. I should have known better. But a girl can't always help herself, and the way I saw it, Sandal is a bad person."

"Why do you say that?"

"Servants see a lot of things. We overhear whispers and low conversations. Sometimes, people speak as if we aren't even there. They say the most outrageous things. I'm ashamed for them."

"And I'm ashamed for you, thief."

"Why are you giving me grief? I've been nothing but cordial to you, have I not?"

"That's only because you want me to help you escape. Well, I have bigger problems."

"You can say that again." Grey Cloak reappeared. Sweat glistened on his face as he pulled the scarf down.

Dyphestive scrambled to his feet and pushed his nose through the bars. "Spill it."

"Everything you said earlier was right. I heard Sandal and Lorry admit to everything. What's worse is they're working for Black Frost," Grey Cloak said. "And worse than that was that Sandal and Lorry kissed."

"Ew," Dyphestive and Tula said.

"I know. You don't ever want to see that. Creepy little—"

Dyphestive seized his brother's cloak. "Will you stop talking and get me out of here, or will I have to do it myself?"

"I will, but we need a plan."

Streak popped his head out. "I have one. I'm a witness. Let me tell Hercullon my side of the story."

Grey Cloak shoved Streak back into the hood. "He won't believe you. He won't believe any of us. That's the problem. But the contest was moved up to tomorrow, and if we don't stop it, he'll be dead, and Dark Mountain will take over."

"We can't let that happen." Dyphestive gave a heavy sigh.

"I agree, but consider this: What if it's meant to happen? What if it happened already?" Grey Cloak asked.

"No." Dyphestive shook his head. "Even so, we have to make it right. We're here for a reason."

"What are you talking about?" Tula asked. "It doesn't

make any sense. How could it have happened already?"
She stared at them. "What do you mean?"

Dyphestive looked at her. "It's a long story. And we don't
have time to talk about it. Grey, how are we going to change
Hercullon's mind? We need proof."

Grey Cloak shrugged. "I'll think of something."

With another sigh, Dyphestive bumped his head
against the bars. His hard skull made a noticeable thump.
Mauk woke up.

19

"Hello." Grey Cloak lifted the scarf over his nose and vanished.

Mauk jumped out of his chair and drew his sword. He rapidly blinked his sleepy eyes and crept forward, poking his sword into the empty air.

Grey Cloak slipped away from the blade and distanced himself.

"Did you see that?" Mauk asked excitedly. "Did you?"

Tula yawned. "What are you talking about, Mauk? I didn't see anything."

"Neither did I." Dyphestive smiled.

Mauk rubbed his hairy face. "Don't take me for a fool. I know I saw someone, a man—an elf." He pointed at Tula. "Like you."

"Maybe it was me." She shrugged her shoulders and eyebrows. "Or maybe you were dreaming."

"Don't play games with me, thief." Mauk's nostrils flared, and he drew in a deep breath. "I can smell treachery. My barbarian blood senses it."

"You aren't a barbarian," Tula stated.

"All the Culpeppers are." Mauk spun around with his sword, striking at the empty air. "I can feel a presence."

"Mauk, you aren't even a Culpepper. You're a guardian. No relation. If you were a Culpepper, you wouldn't be working in the dungeon," Tula added. "Take it easy. Go sit down and resume your nap."

"Don't mock me, dead woman. I know what I saw. An elf!" He took a stab near where Grey Cloak was standing.

Grey Cloak moved aside, poked the Rod of Weapons into Mauk's belly, and sent a charge into the tip.

Bzzzzzt!

Mauk's entire body twitched. His belly rolled like waves.

Grey Cloak reappeared. To his amazement, Mauk was still standing. "Uh-oh."

"I knew it!" Mauk uttered. "Intruder!" He charged.

With the speed of a striking snake, Grey Cloak dodged Mauk's swinging sword, twisted around the large man, and drove the rod into his back, unleashing more wizard fire.

"Aaaargh!" Mauk's sword clattered on the stone floor. He staggered around, walking on wobbly legs, crashed into the bars of a cell, and finally collapsed with his eyes wide open and drool coming out of his mouth.

"Is he dead?" Dyphestive asked.

Grey Cloak waved his hand in front of the man's face. Mauk didn't blink, but he breathed. "I think he's done in for now. I gave him quite a jolt, twice. I believe his belly absorbed the first one. He's stout. I'll say that much for him. Perhaps he is a barbarian."

"Will you let me out of here now?" Dyphestive pleaded.

"Don't be hasty." Grey Cloak rubbed his chin. "We need to think this through."

Dyphestive grabbed the bars and started to pull against them. "Hurk!"

Tula's eyes grew like saucers.

The bars started to bend as Dyphestive's jaw muscles tightened, and his face turned beet red. Steel gave way to brawn, and the bars bowed like metal spoons. He pulled the steel gap wide open and squeezed through.

Grey Cloak gave him a disappointed look. "Those dungeon doors aren't cheap, you know."

"Will you quit wasting time?" Dyphestive started toward the exit.

"Give me a moment. I have an idea. Maybe. Let me check our assets, because I thought of something." He rummaged through his pockets and produced several finger-length potion vials. "Tatiana filled my pouches with these at the Treasure Room. The problem is I don't know what they do. Now, where's that pamphlet she gave me?"

"I don't see how potions are going to help," Dyphestive said. "We'll have to convince Hercullon ourselves."

Tula reached through the bars and plucked a vial out of Grey Cloak's hand.

"Goy, woman, give that back!" he said.

She retreated behind the bars. "Let me out first."

"No."

"A shame, because I can read it." She ran a delicate finger along the gray wax rim. "See, it's written right here. It says fire-breathing."

"It does not." Grey Cloak fished out the small rolled-up scroll Tatiana had given him. "I have a guide right here." He unrolled the scroll until it hit the ground and started rolling across the floor to Mauk's knees. "Zooks. How long is this list?"

Dyphestive looked over Grey Cloak's shoulder and squinted. "The lettering is very tiny."

"It's going to take me all day to look through this." He tried to match the arcane lettering to the lettering on the vial. "I knew I should have paid more attention during Yuri Gnomeknower's training."

Tula gave him a frozen stare.

He caught her glare and said, "Nothing."

She waggled the potion vial. "Once again, I can read it."

"Don't trust her. She's a thief," Dyphestive said.

"What's wrong with that? She didn't steal anything from us."

"She stole your potion."

"Oh, true." Grey Cloak beckoned with his fingers. "Hand it over, Tula."

Tula returned his steely gaze. "You're wasting time." She twisted the cork on the vial, breaking the wax seal, and chugged the potion.

"Nooo!" Grey Cloak whined.

He gave her an incredulous look as she tipped the vial and shook the last few drops onto her tongue.

"What did you do that for?"

"Mmm... spicy." Tula placed the vial in his outstretched palm. She held up a finger. "Give it a moment." A loud gurgling sound started inside her belly. Her lips curled, and she pressed her palm to her flat belly. "Oh my. I feel like I'm going to give birth again. You better stand back."

Grey Cloak and Dyphestive took one long step away from Tula's cell.

A loud belch followed, and a plume of fire erupted from her mouth that melted the bars like snow. Tula stepped outside of her cell, avoiding the dripping molten metal. "Ah, I feel better."

Grey Cloak reluctantly handed her the potion vials. He didn't know quite what to make of the older woman, but she made him a tad uneasy. "You better not deceive us," he warned. "How did you learn to read magic anyway?"

"A good thief can read many things. That's what makes them good." Tula held up a vial and eyed it in the torchlight. The vial's color was dull, but when she shook it, it turned bright blue with shiny silvery swirls within. "Interesting. Lightning bolts. Where did you get these? They're very aggressive."

"That's none of your business," Grey Cloak said.

"I see." She held up another, shook it, and read the lettering engraved in the wax. "Steel skin." She looked at another and another. "Giantus." She eyed it. "Only a dose left. Ah, mending. Very helpful. I'd hold onto that one. Let's see, this one is apparition."

"What does that do?" Dyphestive asked.

"Turns you into a ghost." Tula jiggled another potion. "Hmm... telepathy, another mending potion, sustenance, hah, that will keep your belly full. I don't see how any of these are going to be of much help, but I could take them off your hands and sell them for a lot of money. I know a merchant who would be very interested."

Streak rested his head on Grey Cloak's shoulder. "I'd like to try the lightning bottle. Sounds cool."

Grey Cloak took back several potion vials. He shook the telepathy vial. It turned into a somber green color. He smirked. "I have an idea."

"Which one is that?" Dyphestive asked with a curious look.

"Telepathy, it allows you to read a person's mind." He took back another handful of vials and put them back inside his cloak. "Hand over the other one, Tula."

She gave a sheepish smile. "This potion offers fleetness. I was hoping to keep it."

"Sorry, but you're on your own, dragon breath."

Dyphestive tugged on his shoulder. "Care to get back to your plan? How is reading minds going to help us warn Hercullon?"

"Easy. We aren't going to read his mind. He's going to read ours once he drinks this."

"Ah." Dyphestive's expression brightened.

"Good idea, boss." Streak's pink tongue flicked out of his mouth. "But how are you going to get him to drink it?"

"I'll turn invisible and put it in his ale or something." He pulled the Scarf of Shadows over his nose. "Simple, yes?"

"I can still see you," Dyphestive stated.

"So can I," added Tula.

"Zooks, I forgot. It only works once in the day, and I dispelled it when I revealed myself to Mauk."

"Smooth." Tula put her hands on her hips. "Now what are you going to do?"

"Do you know where Hercullon is now?" Dyphestive asked.

"He went to train."

Dyphestive nodded. "I know where that is." He opened his palm. "Let me have the potion."

Grey Cloak handed it over. "What are you going to do?"

"Pour it down his throat if he won't listen. Let's go."

Tula moved to the door that led to the guard room. She pressed her ear against the door then turned to the brothers. "I'll handle the guards. You two make a run for it."

"No, wait," Grey Cloak said.

Before he could reach her, she started pounding on the door.

"Have you gone mad?"

"Don't worry. I have a plan," she said.

The door cracked open. Someone on the other side said, "What is it, Mauk? Are you hungry again?"

Dyphestive pushed by Tula, manhandled the door, and yanked it open. The guard stumbled inside the dungeon and fell down the steps. He fought to stand, but Grey Cloak zapped him with the Rod of Weapons.

"I really am getting good at this." Grey Cloak spun the rod around his body. "No killing, but it leaves a mark and I'm sure an awful headache."

The second dungeon guard rushed Dyphestive with his sword and unleashed a downward chop. Dyphestive caught the man's wrist in one hand and punched him out with his fist. The burly guard crumpled to the floor. Dyphestive dragged the guard into the dungeon and rolled him down the steps, putting him by the first guard.

He eyed Tula and Grey Cloak. "Come on."

The trio exited, and Tula locked the guards inside the dungeon using the ring of keys. When she turned around, she was facing Grey Cloak and Dyphestive. "What?"

Grey Cloak said, "This is where we part ways, Tula."

"You aren't going to help me escape?" she asked.

"We aren't escaping. You're on your own," Dyphestive replied.

She gave them both a dejected look. "I'm sad, but I'm grateful for your help." She offered an embrace. "Hugs?"

They put up their hands.

"No thanks, sticky fingers," Grey Cloak said.

"Have it your way." She tossed the ring of keys in the air then sprinted between them, up the stairs, and out of sight. "Goodbye," she said, her voice fading as it echoed down the stairwell and died.

"She was strange," Grey Cloak said, "and oddly fast." He looked at his brother. "Lead the way. And remember, we can't be seen."

"I know how to sneak."

"Says the water buffalo. Don't rush it. If the guardians see us, we'll never make it to Hercullon."

Dyphestive nodded. "Oh, we'll make it to Hercullon one way or another. I swear it."

21

Dyphestive hurried through the long corridors and hall-ways on cat's feet. He peeked around every corner before moving to the next one. Grey Cloak remained behind him, little more than a shadow that never spoke a word. They closed in on Hercullon's training arena.

Dyphestive stopped in his tracks. Four guardians lay sprawled on the floor, completely unconscious. The blood brothers hadn't even drawn a weapon. They shared a glance. Grey Cloak shrugged.

Dyphestive resumed the lead, walking over the fallen men like they were logs in the grass. He took the stairs to the lower level of the stronghold and found more men knocked out along the way.

"Mercy," Grey Cloak whispered. He dropped to a knee

and put his hand on a warrior's neck. "He breathes. All their chests rise and fall."

"We need to get to Hercullon quick," Dyphestive said.

He picked up speed and headed down the stairs into the training arena. He spotted Hercullon in the middle of the arena with his back turned away and his arms spread wide. He held metal clubs up like torches in his hands. Drops of sweat rolled down Hercullon's back. A puddle of water formed on the floor beneath his chin.

"What's he doing?" Grey Cloak whispered.

"I can hear you," Hercullon responded in his strong, resonant tone. "And I recognize your voice. You shouldn't have come here, Grey Cloak. You're going to die." He lifted the two clubs in his hands, and his scarred arms bulged with mighty muscles. "I can only assume you killed my guardians along the way. I should have smelled your treachery." He advanced.

Dyphestive blocked his path. "Hercullon, would we have come here if we were guilty? We aren't the traitors. Sandal and Lorry are."

Hercullon's eyes narrowed. "Is that so?" He lashed out and struck Dyphestive in the arm. He blasted Dyphestive in the leg with the other club, knocking him from his feet. "Feel that, boy? That's pain. And more's coming!" He pointed a club at Grey Cloak. "For you!"

"Can't we talk about this?" Grey Cloak backed away

with his rod in his hands. The end flared up with blue light. "I'd hate to hurt a friend."

"Magic." Hercullon spit. "Pah."

Dyphestive dived on Hercullon's ankles. "You have to listen to us. They want you to die."

Hercullon whacked him with his club. "Get off me, or I'll bust your skull open!"

Grey Cloak rammed the Rod of Weapons into Hercullon's chest and sent a strong jolt through it.

Hercullon's eyes glowed with the rod's blue light. He returned a nasty grin. "Elf, I'm going to clobber you to death." He swung.

Grey Cloak jumped away. "Zooks! Did you even feel that?"

"I did. It wouldn't be the first time I felt a lightning bolt, and it won't be the last." Hercullon tried to kick his way out of Dyphestive's grasp. "Let go of me, young fool!"

"Hercullon, please listen. Take this potion." Dyphestive revealed the vial. "Hear our thoughts. Hear Sandal's. We aren't lying."

"A potion?" Hercullon's forehead creased. "You jest. Barbarians don't dabble in magic. Any fool knows that."

"On my life." Dyphestive held it higher. "Take it. Then we'll do as you wish. I'll be your prisoner. But I won't fight you any longer. We are right. You are wrong."

Hercullon gave Grey Cloak a wary look. "And you'll surrender as well?"

Grey Cloak swallowed. "I'd rather not, but I stand by my brother."

"Let me have it." Hercullon dropped his clubs, took the potion, gave it a suspicious look, and twisted off the seal. He poured the contents on the ground. "Fools! What sort of barbarian do you take me for? Guardians!" He bellowed like thunder. The ancient banners hanging from the rafters shook. "Guardians!"

No one came.

Hercullon raised a brow. "They'll be here." He walked over to a stone bench, grabbed a towel, and wiped his face. He placed his hand on his knee and studied the brothers. "I'm disappointed." He drank from a bucket sitting on the floor and wiped the water from his beard. "I knew this day would come. The walls would collapse. The wolves would attack. Good men are undone," he muttered.

A dozen guardians rushed into the training arena. They formed a half circle of spears around the blood brothers.

"You would be wise to surrender peacefully." Hercullon drained the bucket. "My guardians won't hesitate to kill you."

Grey Cloak and Dyphestive lifted their hands over their heads.

"We gave our word." Dyphestive gave Hercullon one long last look. "It is good. It always has been. But I can't say the same about—"

"Silence!" Hercullon punched the stone bench, breaking the corner off. "Take them away!"

The blood brothers both wound up sitting inside a different cell with bars twice as thick as the one Dyphestive had been in before. This time, the guards were tripled. The brothers sat across from one another with their wrists and legs in irons.

"That plan was an epic failure." Grey Cloak put his head between his knees. "I mean, you handed him the potion, and he poured it out. That might have been the most astonishing thing I've ever seen. I thought you would try to hold him down and feed it to him. What were you thinking?"

"I thought he might believe me," Dyphestive said. "When I looked into his eyes, I saw doubt. Not in us, but in Sandal. He wanted to believe us. I know it." He shook his fists. The chains rattled. "I'm a fool!"

"Quiet in there!" Mauk beat the bars with a club. "I hope I'm the one who takes your heads from your shoulders. You'll pay for what you did."

"Why don't you sleep it off, Mauk? You're good at that," Dyphestive said.

Grey Cloak brightened. "Good one, brother. I like hearing that sort of fire from you."

"Don't get used to it." Dyphestive's head dropped. "What are we going to do?"

"We can only do what we can do," Grey Cloak said in whisper. "We tried. But this place is lost. We need to escape. Agreed?"

Dyphestive gave a reluctant nod. "Agreed."

22

Stormy-eyed, Hercullon marched back toward his quarters. The blood brothers had gotten into his head. *Why would the young men risk their lives to warn me?* Their words rang true, and he had a good sense of character when it came to meeting people.

They wanted to save their skins. That's why. Sandal would never betray me.

Sandal called down to him from the top of the stairs. "My love, what is it? What's happened?"

"Our guests escaped. It's been handled." Hercullon noticed Lorry standing beside Sandal with a surprised look on his face. He started up the stairs. "They're back in the dungeon."

Sandal hurried down the steps and met him halfway.

She hooked his arm. "Did they try to kill you? Are they assassins?"

"No." He shook his head. "They made ridiculous claims about my wife." He glanced at Lorry. "And you."

Lorry wrung his hands. "What sort of claims, my lord?"

"Nothing worth mentioning." He let Sandal lead him up the stairs. "We'll deal with them later. I have a fight to prepare for."

"Of course, my love. I hate to see you distraught." Sandal kissed his hand. "Come to our quarters, and I'll soothe you. After all, our champion must be focused for his big victory tomorrow." She added, as if speaking to herself, *Where he's sure to die.*

"What?" Hercullon asked.

Sandal gave him a surprised look. "Pardon me, my love?"

He shook his head. "I thought I heard you say something else."

The old fool is paranoid. Tomorrow his skull will be smashed like an egg, and he'll have no worries anymore. Neither will we, Lorry said, but his lips didn't move.

Hercullon tilted his head and glared at Lorry. "What did you say?"

Lorry blanched. "Nothing, my liege. Is something wrong?"

"Perhaps." Hercullon squeezed his eyes shut. He heard Sandal and Lorry's thoughts swimming in his head.

He's losing his mind.

The old fool will die tomorrow.

The Homestead will soon be ours.

Sandal will be mine forever.

The Culpepper legacy will be destroyed once and for all, after this rotting goat dies.

Hercullon grabbed the rail and pulled himself up the stairs with the weight of the world on his shoulders. His face broke out in a sweat as he tried to block their thoughts but couldn't.

"My love, speak to me," Sandal pleaded. "You don't look well. You're sweating."

He made it to the top of the steps and stood with his chin down. "Those young men, Dyphestive and Grey Cloak, made awful accusations."

"I know." Sandal rubbed his back. "But the elf made inappropriate advances on me. You believe me, don't you?" *You old fool, of course you do.*

"I'm not talking about that. Though he did accuse you of lying." He lifted his eyes to look at them both. "The elf made an outrageous statement. He said the pair of you were lovers."

Lorry let out a nervous laugh and swallowed.

Hercullon's voice grew stronger. "They said you're in league with Dark Mountain, that you plot and scheme my doom."

How would the elf know we're lovers? Sandal thought.

Lorry thought clearly, *We've been plotting and scheming for a very long time, and we won't fail now.*

Hercullon saw the guilt in their eyes as plain as day. It vanished quickly, but it was there, as bright as a shooting star, then gone. His heart became heavy, but the furnace within began to churn.

Sandal hugged his arm. "They're desperate, my love. They will conceive any lie to save themselves." *As would I. After all, I've been doing it for years.*

Hercullon lifted his head. On heavy feet, he moved forward between the two of them. "Come. Let's put this behind us and proceed forward. I have an important day tomorrow."

"Absolutely, my liege. Shall I have the servants draw you a hot bath?" Lorry recommended. *After all, it will be your last one, you noble savage.*

Hercullon laid a heavy hand on Lorry's shoulder. "I would like that. But first—" He grabbed Lorry by the neck and lifted him from his feet. He squeezed his iron fingers around the man's vocal cords. "I'll have the truth!" Using one mighty arm, he shook Lorry like a rag. "Have you been sleeping with my wife?"

Lorry's face turned purple. He chopped at Hercullon's arms to no avail.

Sandal tried to pull Hercullon's arm down. "Have you gone mad, my husband? Let your faithful servant down!"

There was no mistaking the desperation in her thoughts and voice.

"Faithul! What do you know about being faithful?" He squeezed Lorry's neck harder. "In your own words, tell me the truth!"

"I-I-" Sandal said.

Dinah, the Culpeppers' daughter, dressed in leather and fur winter garb, came rushing from her room. "Father, what's going on here? Put Lorry down! You're killing him!"

"Yes," Hercullon said in a robust voice. "I will kill him unless your mother tells the truth!"

"Hercullon, please, don't do this." She sank to her knees and sobbed. "It's true." Tears streamed down her face. "I love him. Not you."

"Mother!" Dinah said in outrage. "How could you?"

"Because your father is a fool!" Sandal gathered her strength and glared up at Hercullon. "You and your barbaric nobility. An alliance with Black Frost is the future of our people. It is our survival! But you want to stand by your traditions, protect those slaving wolves beyond the border." She spit on his boots. "You will get us all killed."

"No, only you and him." Hercullon looked Lorry dead in the eye. "I always knew something stank about you. I could never grasp it until now. You've always served Black Frost's forces, haven't you?"

"Not only have I served," Lorry managed to say. "But I've delighted in it and your wife as well."

Hercullon lifted Lorry above his shoulders. "Perhaps you'll delight in this!" He hurled the man over the balcony.

"Noooo!" Sandal rushed to the railing.

Lorry landed like a cat, glared up at them with eyes that changed into a serpent's, and scurried away.

Sandal's jaw hung.

Dinah stood by her father's side with her dagger out. "I've never seen eyes like that. What was he?"

"Evil of the worst kind. A chameleon."

23

THE MAIN DOOR into the dungeon groaned on its hinges. Mauk, who stood guard in front of Grey Cloak and Dyphestive's cells, turned. His thick eyebrows lifted. He backed up and took a knee with his head down. "Hercullon! I mean, Lord Culpepper! It's an honor!"

Hercullon's mighty frame stepped into full view. He glowered down at the sitting brothers. "It appears you told the truth after all, but how did you get me to drink your potion of telepathy?"

"We didn't." Grey Cloak stood up.

Dyphestive joined him. "What happened?"

"Everything was as you said. I heard their thoughts the same as my own. I couldn't believe what I heard." Hercullon touched his cheekbone. "But when I saw the looks on their faces after I mentioned their affair and alliance with Dark Mountain, I knew."

"I'm sorry," Dyphestive offered.

"No matter. It is I who should offer my apologies and gratitude. It appears that Lorry is a chameleon, a savage, deceitful creature that infiltrated my stronghold and seduced my wife." Hercullon sighed and shook off his sad look. "You shed light on the evil fiend. You have my thanks."

"Did you kill it? Or him?" Dyphestive asked.

Hercullon shook his head. "The search is on, but fiends like that are difficult to detect, even for a barbarian."

"What about Sandal?" Grey Cloak asked.

"She is with Dinah. We'll try to work matters out, but at this time, I have more important matters to attend to. The contest is tomorrow." Hercullon eyed Dyphestive. "I know it is much to ask, but will you still be my champion?"

Before Dyphestive could respond, Grey Cloak spoke up. "Would you free us so I might speak with my brother before he gives you his answer?"

"Of course." Hercullon gestured for Mauk to release the brothers.

Once freed, Grey Cloak pulled Dyphestive aside and spoke in a low voice. "You don't have to do this. Now might not be the right time."

"You know as well as I do that we have to help them

now. Ice Vale needs Hercullon. He's a good man. It will fall to Black Frost without him."

"Did you ever think that perhaps it already has?" Grey Cloak asked.

"Would you allow the Sky Riders at Gunder Island to die if you could stop it?"

Grey Cloak sighed. "Agreed. But you don't know what you're getting into. It sounds dangerous, fighting this barbarian."

"Would you like to fight him for me?"

"No."

"I didn't think so." Dyphestive smirked. "I'll take my chances."

"This is the Arena of Stone," Hercullon said.

Night had fallen, and they'd traveled to the border between the Ice Vale township and the snowy ridges of the Wolves in the Rocks. "Tomorrow, the benches will be filled with thousands of raving people calling for death." He eyed Dyphestive with fire in his gaze. "I love it."

"I can see why. The seats look very comfortable," Grey Cloak remarked.

The three of them, plus Streak, stood on the edge of the twenty-foot wall that overlooked the arena. The entire structure had been hewed out of stone. That included everything from the floor to the walls of the circular ring, and the rows of seats. The rough arena floor had boulders and stones of all shapes and sizes, forming a natural, rocky terrain. In the middle were slabs and boulders that made platforms and ledges ten to twenty feet high. Dark blood stains marred the ground and rocks. The footing appeared loose in many places.

"This is only used every five years?" Dyphestive asked.

"No, we have contests and challenges a few times a year. It keeps the masses entertained. We stand on the south end." He pointed to the opposite side. "That is the north, where the Wolves in the Rocks will enter." He narrowed his eyes. "Can you see them huddled in the shadows, sniffing out their opponent?"

Dyphestive nodded. "I do."

"No doubt they've heard about White Ice's slayer. Knowing they have a new opponent will make them wary." Hercullon pumped his fist in the air and shouted, "We'll bathe in your blood tomorrow, winter hounds! You'll soon see!"

The distant figures hiding in the shadows retreated into the tunnel entrance and disappeared from sight.

"My brethren fear the unknown. Like magic, they fret about what they do not understand. Their ignorance keeps them hiding in their hills, so long as no one provokes them." Hercullon pulled the cork out of a flask and handed it to Dyphestive. "Drink this. It will warm your blood."

Dyphestive took a long swig of the bitter drink. "Eh, I think it will do more than warm my blood. It might rot it."

Hercullon planted his fists on his hips and let out a gusty laugh. He howled above the winds. "Ah ha ha ha!" He took the flask from Dyphestive and stuffed it against Grey Cloak's chest. "Drink with us, elf. It might be your brother's last."

Grey Cloak sniffed the contents and took a sip. "That's awful."

"Hah! That's the best grog a barbarian can buy." He took back the flask and drank. "You'll be fighting Mad Wolf the Berserker. I need to tell you what to do to beat him."

"So, he can be beaten?" Grey Cloak asked.

Hercullon shrugged and drank again.

24

THE ARENA OF STONE'S seats were filled by midday from top to bottom. The citizens of the Ice Vale township, bundled in woolen coats, heavy scarfs, and winter caps, all crammed together on the south side. The sullen-eyed barbarians entered from the north, half-naked in furs and skins. They sat on the snowy stone benches, quiet, never blinking an eye.

A steady snow fell from the sky, covering the arena stones in a new layer of white frosting. The Homestead Guardians carried torches and lit the urns spread out along the arena rim. They kept one hand on their pommels as they passed by the icy gazes of the black-haired barbarians.

Hercullon Culpepper sat on a throne-like stone chair covered in animal pelts. Sandal sat on his right, and Dinah sat on his left. Sandal wore a frown, a glassy look in her eyes.

Grey Cloak and Dyphestive stood nearby, overlooking the arena. The citizens bristled, barely able to contain their excitement. If Dyphestive lost, they would have a new leader, and the betting folk were putting most of their wages against the Culpepper family.

"Do you get the feeling that a giant brawl could break out at any moment?" Grey Cloak asked Dyphestive.

With his eyes fixed on the barbarians, Dyphestive replied, "I'm only concerned about one fight."

"Yes, I can see that. You really are a glutton for punishment, aren't you?"

Grey Cloak watched Hercullon stand to greet dignitaries from across Ice Vale. They shook hands and bumped forearms, offered pleasantries and made short jokes. Sandal didn't engage. The vibrant woman looked like her soul had been ripped out of her.

"It looks like someone's having a bad day."

"Huh?" Dyphestive glanced back at Sandal. "You might want to keep an eye out for Lorry, or the chameleon, whatever that might be."

"I will."

Dinah Culpepper left her seat, came down the stairs, and joined Grey Cloak and Dyphestive. She wrapped her arms around Dyphestive's forearm. "I pray for your victory, and I thank you." She rose up on her tiptoes and kissed his cheek. "You are very brave to do this for my father." She kissed his knuckles. "Be victorious."

"Thank you," Dyphestive said.

Dinah returned to her seat and sat down but not before giving her mother a disappointed look.

With his eyes fastened on Dinah, Grey Cloak said, "You know, being her husband wouldn't be the worst thing you could do. She is very fetching—extraordinarily so."

Dyphestive gave him a dull-eyed look. "I'm going to win, and we're going to get out of here. We have more important things to do."

The skies erupted with the frightening shrieks of dragon calls. Five dragons circled above: three grand dragons and two middlings.

Everyone in the crowd rose from their seats and cheered, waving their arms wildly. Only the stoic barbarians remained seated but with their dark eyes fixed on the sky and every hand on the handle of a blade.

"Zooks. I knew something bad like this might happen." Grey Cloak studied the troubled look on Hercullon's face. "It's going to be difficult to be discreet with you prancing around in that arena."

"They don't know what we look like. Besides, there are a lot of Riskers," Dyphestive said.

"Yes, and we've seen many of them, and they've seen us."

"We were boys then. Much has changed since."

Grey Cloak said, "We can only hope you are right, but Riskers have a sharp eye for detail."

The five dragons circled one more time before landing on the rocky slopes overlooking the arena. Their riders, Riskers, one and all, were indistinguishable in their full suits of blackened platemail armor. The three on the grand dragons dismounted and took a path behind the southern entrance, vanishing below the rim.

Dyphestive's eyes widened. Hercullon caught his worried stare and wandered down to the young men.

"What ails you?" Hercullon asked. "You look as if you've seen a wicked spirit."

"Let's say we've been trying to avoid the Riskers for quite some time," Dyphestive stated.

"Oh, and why is that?" Hercullon asked.

"We—" Grey Cloak started.

Dyphestive cut him off. "We were once slaves in Dark Mountain. We escaped long ago."

Hercullon nodded. "I know you to be honest men. I'll take your secret to my grave, but I suggest you avoid them."

Grey Cloak noticed Sandal leaning toward them. He blocked her view and said to Hercullon, "Try not to mention our names. The lower the profile, the better."

"How will I introduce our champion?"

"Hmm... call him the White Ice Slayer." He eyed Dyphestive. "And try to find a mask."

Dyphestive pulled out the mask of Iron Bones. "How about this one?"

Grey Cloak took it from him and turned it inside out. "If you can't find something else, this will have to do. Try not to make it obvious."

"Maybe you should wear it," Dyphestive suggested.

"I have this." Grey Cloak held up the Scarf of Shadows. "And I can always cover up with something else."

Hercullon squeezed Dyphestive's shoulder and looked him dead in the eye. "Remember what I told you last night. If any man can do this, you can." He waved down a pair of his guardians. "Take him to the chambers below. He'll wait to battle down there."

Dyphestive grasped arms with the slightly larger man. "I will win."

Grey Cloak punched his brother in the arm. "You better."

The Homestead Guardians led Dyphestive into the tunnels toward the rooms below.

"Your brother is difficult to read." Hercullon rubbed his jaw. "I can't tell if he's scared or if he's fearless."

"He's not scared. I promise you that much. Should he be?"

"Even if I were as young as him, I would be."

Something stirred in the tunnel behind the seats above them.

"Ah, the Riskers come. You better lie low," Hercullon suggested. "I must greet them."

"You do that." Grey Cloak took a seat in the crowd.

He felt eyes on him and caught Sandal staring. He averted his eyes and took a quick look at Hercullon and the Riskers he greeted. His heart jumped into his throat the moment he saw Hercullon shaking hands with Commander Shaw, who was accompanied by his son and daughter, Dirklen and Magnolia.

Thunderbolts!

25

MAGNOLIA'S GAZE swept right over his. She turned her head to look again, but he turned away.

I can't believe this!

The last three Riskers he would ever want to see again stood several feet away, and there was no mistaking them. Commander Shaw, the father, was a lean but well-knit man with firm, angular features and a strong jaw. His long brown hair had begun to gray, and his eyes could pierce stone.

Dirklen and Magnolia were twins, each with flowing locks of wavy blond hair and eyes like a bright-blue sky. They stood out in their black armor and carried an air of command about them.

The last time Grey Cloak had seen Commander Shaw, he'd been killed in Monarch City. And Grey Cloak had gotten the upper hand on Dirklen and Magnolia and shoved them through the Time Mural into the world called Bish. He'd thought he'd rid himself of his nemeses forever, yet there they were, in the flesh, but a decade younger than the last time he'd seen them.

He counted on his fingers. The twins should only be a few years older than he was now. He wasn't exactly sure. Either way, they hadn't seen him in the better part of a decade.

I can't let them see my face. It's too much of a risk, and Magnolia's big blue eyes are always probing.

Grey Cloak moved slowly down the row. A firm hand planted itself on his knee and pushed him down.

"Why, Grey Cloak, you look like you've seen a ghost," Tula said. She wore a hooded cloak that covered her eyes and a woolen gray scarf wrapped around her neck. "What's the hurry? You'll miss the show."

"I don't have time to explain. I need to move elsewhere."

She hooked his arm and held him fast with surprising strength. "I wouldn't go anywhere. They're watching you."

He fought the urge to turn. "Who's watching me?"

"The boy and the girl. Well, mostly the girl. She seems very preoccupied with... everything." Tula leaned on his shoulder. "Put your arm around me. Make it look like you're keeping me warm."

"I'd rather not."

"Oh, comfort an old woman, will you?"

He gave her an uncomfortable look but put his arm around her waist. "How old are you?"

"Old enough to be your mother."

"More like my grandmother."

Tula elbowed him. "You should know better than to tease a woman about her age. That's a fine way to show your gratitude."

He arched a brow. "Gratitude for what?"

"Need you ask?" Tula gave him a disappointed look. "Who do you think put the telepathy potion in Hercullon's water?"

"You did that? How? We had the potion."

"No, you thought you had the potion. I kept it. I knew Hercullon wouldn't budge and consume a magic potion. He'd cut off his sword arm first." She smiled. "It wouldn't be the first time a barbarian has done that."

Grey Cloak smirked. "You're a clever fox. I'll give you that. No wonder those guards were already unconscious. Why did you do it?"

"I might be a thief, but I like to be on the right side of matters. I don't want to see Ice Vale fall any more than you do. That's bad for everyone. So, I helped see things along."

"I guess we're even," he said.

"Is that so?"

"Certainly, we freed you, and you repaid us." He moved his hand away from her back. "Now, if you don't mind, I think this is where we part ways. The farther I get from prying eyes, the better."

She nodded. "If you say so. But it's going to appear odd that you give up your seat right before the battle begins."

"I'll take my chances. Besides, shouldn't you be avoiding Sandal's prying eyes? After all, you tried to steal her jewels."

"True." Tula glanced behind her. "But I think she's more preoccupied with you than me."

The crowd came to their feet when the arena master entered the ring. He climbed to the top of the highest rock and spread his arms.

"Go now," she ordered. "They're making introductions."

"No need to tell me twice." Grey Cloak stooped and shoved his way through the surging crowd and up the aisles. He moved to the upper-level seats and found a spot out of sight from Hercullon's box and his guests. He took a breath. "Does it ever get easy?"

Streak snaked his head out a hair. "I don't think so. Oh, look, dragons. We really are in trouble, aren't we?"

"I don't think we could live any other way."

The arena master pushed his arms downward. He was a robust man, more fat than muscle, wearing woolen robes dyed the color of blood and trimmed with animal fur. He spoke with a strong voice that carried from the bottom level all the way to the top and around the ring. The crowd in the stands didn't hesitate to repeat what he said. "Today marks the passing of the Five. Five years ago, our champion, Hercullon Culpepper, battled Zulamax the Dreadful to a bitter but victorious end!"

The crowd erupted in a chorus of thunderous cheers. They pumped their fists in the air, screaming and shouting at the top of their lungs. "Hercullon! Hercullon! Hercullon!"

Hercullon stood, thrust his arm in the air, and resumed his seat.

The hard-eyed Wolves from the Rocks remained seated, like a pack of wolves waiting for their alpha to tell them to attack.

"Today," the arena master said, "a new era is in the fold. The Wolves from the Rocks have a new champion, Mad Wolf the Berserker!"

Without hesitation the people of Ice Vale booed, hissed, and gave their thumbs down.

The arena master lifted his voice. "But Ice Vale has a new champion of its own. A young warrior of great renown whom we've come to fondly know as the White Ice Slayer!"

Cheers, whistles, and applause filled the stadium.

"Champions!" the arena master called out. "Come forth! Let the Contest begin!"

26

Dyphestive couldn't believe his ears. The crowd roared like a crashing waterfall. He stood at the gate, stripped down to his trousers, his mask in hand, and watched the metal door split open. He took a deep breath.

One step at a time, he wandered toward the opening. The two guardians posted at the gate gazed upon him.

"Victory or death," one said.

"You're the champion of us all," said the other.

Holding the mask in his crushing grip, he lifted it before his face and stared into its haunting eyes. "I have a feeling I'm going to need Iron Bones today." He pulled the mask over his head and adjusted it. A coldness fell over his body. He walked into the sunlight and stood before the howling crowd.

"I give you your champion, people of Ice Vale!" the

arena master hollered. "He slays giants, ettins, some say he even slays dragons! The future lies in his fists. Our lives rest on his broad shoulders. Will you be victorious, White Ice Slayer?"

Dyphestive moved deeper into the arena and climbed the rocks piled on the south end. He didn't see any sign of Mad Wolf, but Hercullon, his family, and his guests sat in the box in the stands behind him. He noted Commander Shaw, Dirklen, and Magnolia, who looked upon him with mild amusement. He saw no sign of Grey Cloak.

The arena master lifted his arms high and dropped them suddenly, quieting the crowd. "I see your eyes searching the gate, waiting to see the challenger, a warrior of great renown in the Rocks, a fighter that has never failed. Where are you, Mad Wolf the Berserker?"

People leaned over the arena wall, on one another's backs and shoulders, craning their necks toward the northern entrance. Silence fell over the stadium.

The grinding of metal hinges sounded as the guardians pulled the north gate open. They remained safely on the other side of the gate facing the shadows in the tunnel. Mad Wolf the Berserker eased out of the tunnel. The silence was broken by the whispers and gasps of the crowd as their jaws dropped.

Mad Wolf stood every bit of seven feet tall, broad shouldered and deep chested. The seasoned man wore a long fur cloak with wolves' heads on the shoulders and leather bracers. He had nasty pink scars on his albino skin. His wild hair, covering his ears and stopping at his neck, was as black as coal. His big eyes were like wildfires. His flat nose flared. Cords of muscles twitched in his arms and legs as he moved like a great cat and stood upon the icy rocks in bare feet.

The Wolves from the Rocks started to chant and cheer as Mad Wolf removed his cloak and slung it to the ground. He crouched down, lifted his face to the sky, and bayed like a wolf. His brethren joined him. The sound grew louder, and the dragons roared in return.

Dyphestive glanced back at Hercullon. The man's brow furrowed, and his fists clenched the arms of his chair. He gave the older barbarian a nod and remembered what the king had taught him.

Weapons lay among the rocks, hidden and buried in the dirt, covered by the snow. They were made of stone, wood, and crude metal. In many cases, Hercullon had been forced to kill a man by crushing his neck with his bare hands. No one could leave without the other being dead.

The arena master announced, "Let the contest begin!" He jumped down from the rocks, rolled forward, bounced to his feet, and ran inside the southern chamber tunnel.

The gates closed and were secured with chains, leaving Dyphestive and Mad Wolf the Berserker alone in the arena.

Dyphestive clenched and relaxed his fingers, waiting. *Let the barbarian come to me.*

Mad Wolf hopped down from his perch on the rocks and disappeared among the heaps of stone. He howled, and his voice echoed throughout the stadium.

Dyphestive searched the grounds from behind his mask. He saw his frosty breath before his eyes. Even if the barbarian was a natural, he found it hard to believe the man could kill him with his bare hands. He knew it would take more than that to defeat him. He would need a weapon of some sort.

The crowd gasped and pointed at Mad Wolf whenever he appeared in the odd channels made from the rocks below. Dyphestive heard digging and more savage grunts and howls coming from the savage man.

"Booo!" the people screamed. "Booo!"

Someone threw an ice ball at Dyphestive and hit him in the side of the face. "Get down there and fight!"

The citizens of Ice Vale came unhinged. They screamed and shouted at the top of their lungs and launched more ice balls at Dyphestive. He brushed himself off.

Mad Wolf climbed up the rock behind him and pounced on his back. The savage put him in a headlock, drove him to his knees, and squeezed his head like a melon.

The barbarians came to their feet, howling like savages.

27

GREY CLOAK COULDN'T BELIEVE his eyes. Mad Wolf scrambled up the rocks like he'd been fired from a crossbow. Both men tumbled off the stone, hit the ground, and vanished behind the rocks.

Anvils!

"That's one big man," Streak commented. "I've never seen a man so large move so fast before. Dyphestive is slow by comparison."

"Don't say that." Grey Cloak pushed his way through the crowd, closer to the arena. A feeling of dread had overcome him the moment Mad Wolf had appeared. He was an older, seasoned man, covered in scars and brawn, who moved with the ease of a jungle cat. If he were truly a natural, Dyphestive might be in for more than he'd bargained for. "I need to help."

"You can't go in there. It will ruin everything. Have faith in Dyphestive. He can take it," Streak offered.

Grey Cloak made it to a spot where he could glimpse Dyphestive being choked to death. Mad Wolf was on top of Dyphestive, his fingers locked on the younger man's neck, and he squeezed with all his might. Blue veins rose in his white arms. Dyphestive punched Mad Wolf in the jaw, snapping the man's head sideways. Mad Wolf grinned and spit out a tooth.

The audience jumped out of their seats.

"Fight him, brother!" Grey Cloak shouted.

Dyphestive exploded into action. He hammered his fists into Mad Wolf's jaw in a club-like fashion. Mad Wolf sprang away. With blood dripping out of his mouth, he made a frightening howl. He reached down and picked up a boulder half his size. He hefted it onto his shoulders like a bundle of straw.

"Move, Dyphestive!" Grey Cloak didn't know if his brother could hear a thing.

The crowd screamed incoherently. Dyphestive rubbed his neck and coughed inside of his mask.

"Move!"

Dyphestive turned in time to see Mad Wolf bringing down the rock. He rolled away from the rock, avoiding it by inches. Mad Wolf hurdled over the stone in a single leap. He whaled on Dyphestive like a drum. His fists smacked into flesh with one hard blow after another.

The crowd could hear it all.

Smack! Smack! Smack!

Dyphestive collapsed chest-first on the ground. Mad Wolf kicked his ribs several times. The barbarian reached down and picked up the stone again, raised it far over his head, and prepared to deliver the final blow. The crowd gasped. The barbarians roared in triumph.

Grey Cloak screamed, "Noooo!"

Dyphestive groaned. Mad Wolf had stunned him with speed and raw power and had made a punching bag out of him. Every blow rocked his innards. He felt every bit of it.

Shake it off. He'd been through the Flaming Fence before. The Doom Riders had put him through it. *Shake it off!* He started to see red. *You've been through worse.*

He rolled over in time to catch the stone crashing down on his chest. "Aaaargh!"

Mad Wolf flexed his muscles and howled in triumph. He roared along with the barbarian crowd. The people from the township deflated into their seats. The barbarians stood on their seats beating their chests and letting out wild shouts.

Enough. With one arm, Dyphestive shoved the boulder off his chest. He sat up, bloodied and bruised, like a man rising from the dead.

Everyone in the stands fell silent. Mad Wolf's howling ceased. He turned toward Dyphestive and tilted his head. His nostrils flared. He dashed into the rocks and disappeared.

"Brother!" Grey Cloak shouted from the stands. He stood on the edge of the arena's wall with his hands cupped to his mouth. "How are you holding up?"

"I survived the first assault, but he's fast and as strong as a bull." Dyphestive adjusted his mask.

"Can you handle it?"

"I don't have a choice." Dyphestive checked the footprints in the snow and gave chase at a slow pace.

With renewed energy, the citizens of the township started chanting, "Slay the Wolf! Slay the Wolf! Slay the Wolf!"

Dyphestive had no intentions of slaying anyone, but if it came to a matter of survival, he wouldn't have a choice. Mad Wolf had almost choked him to death once. He'd felt his vision dim. It stirred his fear and warmed his blood.

I'm not going to let that happen again.

He spotted a patch in the ground where the dirt had been dug out underneath the snow. An impression of a weapon was left in the empty spot.

Horseshoes.

Mad Wolf came out of nowhere and busted Dyphestive in the back of the head with a club made of stone. The club snapped in half.

Dyphestive stumbled forward with stars in his eyes. He felt a blade drive into the flesh behind his shoulder blade. "Gah!" He twisted around and snared Mad Wolf by the hair on his head. He yanked the man backward and punched him as hard as he could in the ribs.

The wind went out of Mad Wolf. His body doubled over, and he howled no more. He took punch after punch that Dyphestive unleashed with fury. Drops of blood fed the snow. Mad Wolf fell as hard as Dyphestive hit and lay face-first on the ground.

The masses in the arena hollered at the top of their lungs, "Kill him! Kill him! Kill him!"

Dyphestive shook his head. "No."

28

"Booooo!"

"Booooo!"

"Booooo!"

The people in the stands made their intentions clear. They wanted Mad Wolf dead. Dyphestive wouldn't kill a man in cold blood. He'd pummeled the barbarian into submission. Victory had been achieved.

From the stands, Hercullon shook his head. His hard stare pierced Dyphestive, the message clear in his eyes. *Finish him.*

Mad Wolf might have been down, but he wasn't out. He stood. His dark eyes blazed like wildfires. His muscular chest heaved. He slavered and spit blood.

"The berserker is cut loose!" someone in the crowd shouted.

Dyphestive stepped toward the towering man and watched the blue veins rise under his skin like worms. Mad Wolf charged. Dyphestive braced for impact. Their bodies collided, hard muscle smacking together.

Dyphestive was lifted into the air and thrown. His back crashed into the rocks. "Guh!"

A flurry of punches and kicks followed, overwhelming him. Mad Wolf beat the daylights out of him. He grappled the barbarian's arms. Mad Wolf pulled free and hammered Dyphestive's face with his fist.

Whap! Whap! Whap!

Mad Wolf gripped him in a powerful chokehold and bit his ear.

"Aaaargh! Get off me!" Dyphestive planted a boot in the man's gut and sent him flying. Warm blood ran down his face. His blood ran hot. He was in a fight with a natural-born killer that was as wild as an animal. He lifted his fists and beckoned to the barbarian. "Bring it, dog!"

Mad Wolf rushed him like a tornado. The bigger and quicker man scooped Dyphestive up and tossed him across the arena. He pounced on Dyphestive's back and beat him in the head with a rock.

Dyphestive twisted underneath Mad Wolf and seized the man's wrists.

The barbarian headbutted him. *Whack! Whack! Whack!* Cartilage cracked. Fresh blood fed the snow. Mad Wolf beat Dyphestive with relentless fury. He grabbed Dyphestive by the leg and dragged him across the arena, making a messy path in the snow.

Everyone in the stands howled with bloodlust. They screamed for more.

It took everything Dyphestive had in him to fend off the furious assault. Mad Wolf had bitten his ear half off through the mask. His nose was busted and there was no telling what else. He hurt all over. He fought on, punching back and kicking, only to be overwhelmed again.

Mad Wolf stomped his ribs, kicked his groin, punched his face.

Dyphestive tried to crawl away only to have Mad Wolf grab his ankle and twist it until bone gave away. *Snap!*

"Aaaaaargh!" he cried out.

The barbarian stuffed a fist in his throat and continued to rip him to pieces.

Hold on! Fight back!

In the recesses of his mind, he remembered what Hercullon had told him. "You don't have to beat him. You have to outlast him."

Mad Wolf grabbed him in a one-armed chokehold. He dragged Dyphestive up the rocks in the center of the arena where everyone could watch him beat the young warrior mercilessly.

"Get out of there!" Grey Cloak screamed. He'd never seen his brother suffer so much. Mad Wolf was tearing him apart like cooked chicken. He started to climb over the wall.

Tula grabbed him by the arm and pulled him back. "You can't do that! They'll all rip you apart."

"I'm not going to watch him die!"

"Have faith. Your brother is strong. Believe in him," Tula urged.

"What do you know about it?" He pushed her away. "I'll do what I have to do. I'll do it my way." He lifted the scarf over his nose and vanished.

Without a word, he jumped the wall and landed in the arena. He glanced up and saw Tula look right at him, disappointment in her eyes. He ran to save his brother, but an unseen force lifted him off his feet.

"Uh, what's happening, boss?" Streak asked in his ear. "Are we flying?"

Grey Cloak swam in the air. The unseen force pulled him back toward the wall and placed him in his spot beside Tula.

She yanked his scarf down. "You need to listen to your elders!"

He reappeared, but no one in the stands of raving people took notice. "Why did you do that?" he yelled. "And how did you do that?"

She wiggled a potion in front of his face. "You missed one. Well, maybe two."

Grey Cloak clenched his jaw, turned away, and watched Mad Wolf pound Dyphestive's face into the rocks. "If he dies, I'll bury you."

Mad Wolf ripped Dyphestive's mask off. He slung the bloody rag down, put Dyphestive in a headlock, and let out a bloodcurdling howl.

Immense pressure built in Dyphestive's skull. His heart beat in his ears, and the world began to turn black. *Hang on. Fight back.*

Mad Wolf ramped up the pressure.

Dyphestive's ears popped. His neck muscles tightened like steel bars. He thrust his head back. Reaching behind him, he pried Mad Wolf's iron fingers from his neck. He battled on through excruciating pain.

One at a time.

He grabbed one finger and bent it back until it cracked. He hooked another appendage and twisted away.

Mad Wolf howled. He forced Dyphestive's neck farther down.

Dyphestive pushed his head back and flexed his shoulders. "Aaaaaaargh!"

Mad Wolf matched his intensity with boundless strength.

Dyphestive fought on. "Grrrrrrrrrrr!" He matched savagery with savagery, breaking another finger.

Without warning, Mad Wolf slammed Dyphestive down onto the stone.

"No!" Dyphestive drew his knee underneath him. He tried to stand on both feet, disregarding his bad ankle. "No!"

Mad Wolf's strong grasp started to fade. Dyphestive's inner fire turned on. He busted out of Mad Wolf's arms. The barbarian's limbs sagged. The veins in his arms faded. His jaw hung open and his chest heaved. He wobbled on his legs. The berserker's eyes cooled.

Dyphestive walloped Mad Wolf in the gut. The man doubled over. A hard uppercut knocked the savage off his feet, sending him flying off the top rock, where he crashed in the snow.

It was over. Dyphestive had outlasted the berserker's rage. Though his body ached all over, he still had some fight in him.

The crowd chanted, "Death! Death! Death! Death!"

He caught Dirklen and Magnolia staring at him. They spoke to one another and pointed. He reached down, picked up his mask, and put it on. Then he turned, faced the Wolves in the Rock, and gave them a thumbs down.

The crowd erupted like a volcano.

29

"I TOLD YOU HE WOULD PREVAIL," Tula said.

Grey Cloak caught his breath. "How could you know? And how can you see me when I'm invisible?"

"I told you before. I have a strong sense of such things."

"Well, we aren't out of the bonfire yet. He still has to finish off Mad Wolf. He won't do it." Grey Cloak frowned.

"How can you be sure?"

"I know him."

"They won't let him out of there alive," Tula said. "If he doesn't kill the barbarian, he'll surely die."

"No need for the reminder. I know what's coming." Grey Cloak had caught Dirklen and Magnolia fastening their gazes on Dyphestive the moment Mad Wolf had pulled the hood off. They were still talking and appeared to have shared the information with their father, Commander Shaw. "We might have a problem."

Tula followed his eyes. "Oh, the Riskers. Yes, they're always a problem. Wherever they go, treachery follows."

"I'm sure you know a lot about treachery."

Hercullon Culpepper rose, and the people quieted.

"White Ice Slayer, you must finish the battle, or you will be finished yourself."

"Finish him. Finish him. Finish him," the crowd chanted quietly.

Dyphestive shook his head. "I won't kill an already-defeated man. If you want to finish him, you will have to finish him yourself."

"I told you he wouldn't kill him," Grey Cloak said.

"Listen to me. You're the champion. This is the rule. When you agree to fight, you agree to fight to the death. It has always been so, and can be no other way," stated Hercullon. "You dishonor your opponent. You dishonor the arena. Finish him."

"You are the ruler. Change the rules," Dyphestive said.

One of the barbarians stood up among his kin. He wore a cap of black wolf fur that matched his jet-black hair and beard. He spoke with a biting tongue and authority. "What is wrong with your dog's tongue, Hercullon? If he does not finish it, you forfeit!"

The barbarians shouted, "Aye!"

"Silence, Black Wolf! He's my champion. I'll do the talking," Hercullon fired back.

"To live would be to live without honor. My son won't live like that!" Black Wolf drew his sword. "Have your champion finish the contest, forfeit, or you will have war on your hands!"

"There must be a better way to end this contest." Grey Cloak studied the prickly atmosphere.

The citizens were on the edge of their seats with nervous looks in their eyes. Many of them started to sneak out.

"What must be done, must be done," Tula said. "It's nearly impossible to change such traditions. Besides, Black Wolf wants to be the ruler of Ice Vale. He's always wanted it for himself."

Black Wolf spoke. "What is it going to be, Hercullon? Do you forfeit?" He tapped his blade against the palm of his hand. "Or do you die?"

Hercullon pulled back his shoulders and held his head high. "My champion is right. Enough blood has been shed in the arena. We have a clear victor." He pointed at Dyphestive. "And it is him! Go back to your hills, Black Wolf. The day is done. Take your champion with you, so you can fight again."

"Interesting. Perhaps cooler heads will prevail," Tula commented.

Sandal Culpepper rose and stood by her husband, as

did her daughter.

Grey Cloak smirked. "I think you might be right."

In the wink of a lash, Sandal's eyes switched to that of a serpent's. She plunged a dagger between Hercullon's ribs and smiled, a snake tongue flicking out of her mouth.

Hercullon fell back into his seat.

Black Wolf raised his steel. "Wolves, attack!"

"Noooooooo!" Dyphestive watched in horror as Sandal stabbed her husband and turned the blade.

Hercullon's eyes grew big. He sank back into his seat.

For a moment, a hush fell over the pie-eyed people, who soaked in the assassination. Their shocked faces turned to anger.

The howling Wolves from the Rocks came.

It all came together in Dyphestive's mind. Hercullon's enemies had no intention of letting him live out the day, win or lose. His time to rule had come to an end.

The people fled for the tunnels.

Homestead Guardians moved quickly and blocked the advance of the barbarians charging through the stands. Metal clashed against metal. Axes came up and went down. The guardians were fewer in numbers. Soon, they would be slaughtered.

Dyphestive stood on one bad leg, searching the stands

for his brother. He found something else. Commander Shaw's fingertips glowed with white fire. Tendrils of energy blasted into the fleeing people of Ice Vale.

The middling dragons in the southern hills shot streams of flame that swallowed the people in fire. Fur and skin turned to ash. Greasy smoke rolled into the sky. The grand dragons took flight, heading toward the town. They would turn the entire settlement into flames if someone didn't stop them.

"Nooooo!" Dyphestive witnessed peace come to an end.

War had arrived, and no one had seen it coming. The peaked Hercullon sagged in his throne, his chin against his chest. The days of the Culpeppers were over.

Dyphestive stood alone in the arena on a broken ankle. The barbarians swarmed the stands. Innocent citizens fled the slaughter. Stalwart guardians battled for their lives.

Grey Cloak soaked it in.

"Ice Vale is lost," Tula said. "We must find safety."

"No." Grey Cloak calculated the odds of survival. "If I know my brother, he won't go anywhere." He watched the Riskers and their dragons crawl into the top levels of the arena and attack. "We have to stop this."

"You're mad!"

Grey Cloak pressed a healing vial into her palm. "Take this to Hercullon. You might be able to save him. Find a way to get him to safety."

"What are you going to do?"

He tapped the Rod of Weapons against his temple. "I'll think of something. Now go."

He set his eyes on Commander Shaw. The older Risker used wizard fire to mow through people in his way as he marched, with his son and daughter by his side, toward the top of the arena. Their grand dragons returned and landed in the rocks. The three of them climbed back onto their beasts, who launched into flight.

"Ha!" Grey Cloak watched them soar higher. "They have other plans." He searched for his brother. "Dyphestive!"

Dyphestive climbed down the rocks. He fell to the ground, landing with a grimace. "What?"

"Can you walk?"

"No, but I can hop."

Barbarians tossed their weapons into the arena and climbed into the pit. With bloodlust in their eyes, they snatched up their weapons and raced toward Dyphestive.

Grey Cloak leaned over the arena wall. "You aren't going to outrun them! Come this way. Hurry!"

Dyphestive hopped toward him.

"Streak, buy us some time, will you?" Grey Cloak asked.

Streak crawled up onto Grey Cloak's head and spread his wings. "Gladly." He dove into the arena, sped toward the barbarians, and unleashed a stream of fire.

The barbarians were consumed in flame. Weapons bared, they kept running toward Dyphestive, screaming their lungs out. With bodies on fire, and skin peeling from their flesh, they attacked.

Streak backtracked and zoomed by Grey Cloak. "Those men are crazy. I better give them another blast."

The flaming savages descended on Dyphestive, but their speed slowed, and some fell along the way. One of the barbarians carried a battle axe. His back was on fire, and he attacked with reckless abandon, bringing the weapon down.

Dyphestive grabbed the axe handle and leveled the warrior with a hard punch in the jaw. The barbarian lay on the ground, knocked out and burning. "I'll be fine." Dyphestive wrist-spun the axe. He set his eyes on another coming wave. "There's only a score or so."

The barbarians were busting through the guardians' defenses and making their way toward Grey Cloak. They would overtake him in moments. His brother would be overrun. With nowhere to turn, he jumped into the arena.

Tula rushed to Hercullon's side and found Dinah Culpepper trying to bandage his wound with a ceremonial towel. She saw no sign of Sandal or the chameleon that had taken her form.

"Let me help," Tula said.

Dinah shoved her back. "Get away from him. I don't know you!"

Hercullon gave a ragged sigh. His broad face turned ashen, and his eyes were bloodshot with black around the rims.

"Listen to me. He bleeds, and he's been poisoned. I have something that might remedy that." She showed the vial of mending. "I'm giving this to you. Whether or not you choose to use it is up to you."

"My father would rather die than use magic. A true warrior can survive on his own."

Tula grabbed Dinah's wrist and squeezed it. "Watch your father die then!"

Hercullon coughed. Fresh blood spattered his lips.

"Father, forgive me." Dinah sobbed, twisting the wax seal from the bottle.

Sandal Culpepper came out of nowhere and dove at her daughter, screeching at the top of her lungs in a man's voice, "Noooo!"

The women rolled down the benches in a tangle of limbs. They tumbled to the bottom of the stands, pulling each other's hair out.

Tula watched with bated breath as the potion vial fell from Dinah's fingers. It bounced on the bench and was kicked down the seats by the panicked crowd. She squeezed Hercullon's cold hand. "Hang on, strong one!"

The vial lay on a bench three rows down. A stampede of screaming people raced straight for it.

She dove with her fingers stretched out. The tips of her fingers grazed the vial and knocked it down between the rows. She covered the spot with her body.

People ran right over her.

"Oof! Ugh!" she groaned. "Oh! Who is wearing heels in this sort of weather?" Banged up and bruised, Tula crawled out of her position. She spotted the vial and snatched it from the ground.

Sandal had Dinah pinned beneath her. A long, forked tongue shot out of Sandal's mouth and wrapped around Dinah's throat. The daughter of Hercullon choked and gagged.

"Chameleon!" Tula shouted. She held out the vial. "Looking for this?"

The chameleon punched Dinah in the face and released her. He stood and transformed into the man they called Lorry. He swept his greasy hair away from his serpentine eyes. "Let me have it, thief." He advanced up the steps. "Hercullon must die so we can all live. Stay out of this and be on the victorious side, or die with the conquered."

Tula nodded. "Is there any money in it for me?"

"More than you can imagine," Lorry the chameleon said.

"Perfect." Tula tossed the vial high in the air.

Lorry's snake eyes glanced up.

Tula opened her mouth, and flames consumed the chameleon.

He burned alive, squalling and screaming, transforming into countless shapes and forms. "Fire cannot kill me!" Lorry shouted. "Your ruse is your doom—*urk!*"

Dinah Culpepper shoved her dagger into his back.

Tula caught the potion. Her flames from the fire-breathing potion went out. "Perfect timing." She watched the lights go out in Lorry the chameleon's eyes. He fell in a heap of flames. She tossed the vial to Dinah. "Give this to your father, quick."

"Thank you." Dinah bounded up the rows toward her father.

Tula turned toward the shouts and screams. Dragons and Riskers came from above, and barbarians closed in from below. She took a deep breath. "This is going to be messy. Should I stay or go? What's an elf to do?"

31

"TAKE THIS." Grey Cloak offered Dyphestive a potion vial.

They had their backs to the wall, and the barbarians were closing in.

Dyphestive took it in hand. "What is it?"

"A mending potion. Hurry!" He stood in front of his brother and fired up the tip of the Rod of Weapons.

The Wolves from the Rock slowed their charge and came forward, weapons out and crouching down.

"Bottoms up!" Dyphestive guzzled it down. "Do you think it will fix my ankle?"

"It should fix anything." He spun his weapon around and gave a warning. "Back up, savages, or I'll make your skulls explode!" He fired a ball of energy into the nearest one.

The barbarian jumped ten feet backward and rolled on the ground.

Streak dropped out of the sky and shot flames from his mouth, setting three barbarians on fire.

They rolled through the snow, fighting the fire that ate their flesh.

"I can't do this all day!" he said as he flew over the brothers. "You might want to come up with a better plan. There's too many!"

Three barbarians rushed forward.

Dyphestive stepped in front of his brother. "I'll handle this."

He cocked back his axe and turned into a sideways swing. His blade passed right through the barbarians and their blades passed right through him. They continued to attack one another in an onslaught, but no one was hitting a thing.

"Grey Cloak, what's happening?"

Grey Cloak blocked a barbarian's sword chop on his staff. He punched the spear end into the wild warrior's chest. "I think I gave you the wrong potion."

Dyphestive stood in the midst of the attacking horde, looking at himself. "What did you give me?"

"Apparition!" Grey Cloak leapt over the heads of three barbarians in a single bound. "You're a ghost now."

"Interesting. But how am I supposed to fight?"

Grey Cloak stuck two men in the back and clobbered

the third in the head. "I don't know! Now I have to fight them all!"

"What am I supposed to do?"

"They're barbarians. Think of something!" Grey Cloak ran from the pack of raving men.

He moved to higher ground and pierced the hand of one climbing behind him. He leapt from one stack of stones to the other. The barbarians chased him like a pack of white apes.

"Streak, I could use a little help!"

Streak swooped down and sprayed the barbarians with smoke. "I told you I was out of juice!"

The blanket of smoke allowed Grey Cloak to navigate away from the horde. He dropped down from the rocks, landed behind a barbarian, and stuck the man in the back. The barbarian spasmed, dropped his sword, and fell.

"Keep spitting that smoke! It's helping!" The haze didn't hinder Grey Cloak at all. He could hear the barbarians scuffling and grunting between the rocks. He slipped into a crevice, waited, and gored another man in the back. "They fall like great timbers."

Dyphestive shouted at the top of his lungs, "Come and get me, savages!"

Grey Cloak popped out of the smoky lair in time to see a pair of barbarians charging his brother. Dyphestive braced himself for the attack. The barbarians passed right through him and smashed into the wall. Dyphestive walked away with the axe slung over his shoulder, almost smiling. A barbarian dove through him. Two more collided.

"Brilliant!" Grey Cloak said.

A bloodthirsty cry caught his ear. He looked up in time to see a barbarian jump on top of him. They crashed into the snow and rolled through the blood and dirt.

"I'm going to cut your ears off, elf, and make a necklace!" the barbarian said.

Grey Cloak put a knee in the man's gut and tried to shove him off. More barbarians piled on top of him, the load of men overwhelming him. They crushed him underneath their brawny weight. He was pinned down, unable to move, with sweaty savages all over him. *This is not the way I want to go.* He cried out, "Dyphestive, do something!"

Dyphestive watched his brother get overrun in a tide of musclebound barbarians. They crushed him in knot of limbs and sinew that punched, kicked, and poked at him.

"Get off of him!" he cried out. He tried grabbing a man to pull him away, but his fingers passed right through the body.

"Ha ha ha, it's over, ghost!" said Black Wolf, the leader of the Wolves in the Rock. "Your mystical tricks have come to an end." He swung his long sword off his shoulder and pointed it at Dyphestive. "And when you become flesh and blood, I'll run you through."

"Take me. Spare him," he pleaded.

"We are the Wolves from the Rocks. We don't spare anybody." Black Wolf flexed his mighty arms, lifted his eyes to the sky, and let out an earsplitting howl. "Oooowuuuuul! Ice Vale is ours, now and forever!" He spotted Streak circling in the sky. He pointed his sword at Streak then to his men with short bows positioned in the stands. "Archers, kill that little dragon! We feast on dragon flesh tonight!"

32

THE CLOAK of Legends buffered some of the barbarians' blows and cuts. The ones it didn't absorb, Grey Cloak felt every bit of. "Ooof!"

One of the brutes connected a foot with his belly. A blade sliced across his cheek.

I have to get out of this!

He tried to worm his way out and make a run for it. Every time he squirmed free, strong, clutching hands brought him down again and pummeled him.

They're going to kill me.

Clinging to the Rod of Weapons, he reached down deep, summoned his wizardry, and let it build inside him. His body burned like fire from head to toe. He let the power loose.

Boooomph!

Bodies of barbarians went flying in all directions. They slammed into rocks, hit the arena wall, and skipped through the snow.

Grey Cloak rose to one knee. Steam came off his cloak, and the snow around him melted. He propped himself up on the Rod of Weapons and trembled.

"Brother, you live!" Dyphestive shouted.

"Aye, but I'm not sure I like it." Everything in his body tingled with pain. He struggled to stand. "I can hardly stand. I could use a hand."

Dyphestive's hand passed right through him. "I can't. I'm useless."

Most of the barbarians were down and out. A few regained their feet, shook their heads, and stumbled through the snow.

Black Wolf stood on the rocks, shouting orders. "Archers!" He pointed to Grey Cloak and Dyphestive. "Kill them!"

Arrows cut through Dyphestive's body and bounced off Grey Cloak's cloak. They made a run for it into the catacombs of rock.

Grey Cloak huddled down in a niche and broke out in a cold sweat. "I feel awful."

Arrows whistled over their heads and clacked off the rocks.

Dyphestive peeked out from cover, and an arrow whizzed through his face. "That's an odd sensation. If we can reach the tunnels, we can make a run for it. Hmmm, but the doors are chained shut."

"And you won't be able to run on your busted ankle."

"You gave me the wrong potion. How long will this last? And I can hop fast."

"I don't know." Grey Cloak fumbled through his pockets. His tired eyes couldn't tell which potion was which. He squinted. "How many of them are out there?"

"Scores are in the stands, but they're moving into the township. I can see plumes of smoke in the distance. It looks like Black Wolf wants to finish us off with the few men he has left."

"Where's Streak?"

Dyphestive craned his neck. "I don't see him."

"Probably hiding. Smart." Grey Cloak winced. They were running out of options, and he could barely keep his eyes open. Summoning his wizardry had drained him. "Well, brother, try not to look when they kill me."

"Don't say that." Dyphestive's eyes grew. "On second thought, how do you feel about being eaten alive?"

"What are you talking about?" Grey Cloak tried to climb to his feet, pushed up, and slid back down again. "Ugh, everything hurts. Tell me what it is."

"It looks like the Riskers joined the barbarians in the hunt."

He looked up at his brother. "Magnolia and Dirklen?"

"No, the middling dragons. They're crawling out of the

stands. It appears they've taken an interest in us." Dyphestive gave him a solemn look. "It's been a really bad day, hasn't it?"

"Don't start complaining now. After all, this was your idea." He pulled back the folds of his cloak and dug into one of his pockets. "If we're going to go out, we don't have to go alone."

"Well, they can't kill me, at least, not at the moment," Dyphestive said. "But on the lighter side, soon enough, you might be an apparition like me—or Dalsay."

"Funny. You know, you find the oddest times to develop your sense of humor." Grey Cloak lifted the Figurine of Heroes. The black faceless carving of a man was as smooth as jade and cool in his hands. "Say hello to our little friend."

"And if this doesn't go our way?" Dyphestive inquired.

"Then I suppose someone else will have to save the world."

The approaching barbarians were engulfed in an explosion of bright flames. Men screamed.

"What was that?" Grey Cloak asked.

"One of the middling dragons attacked the barbarians," Dyphestive said in disbelief. "Now it's attacking the other Risker!"

"This I have to see." He took a deep breath, locked his numb fingers on the rocks, and pushed up with his knees.

The middling dragons were in full battle. One of the

Riskers was tossed from his saddle. The other Risker fired arrows into the attacking dragon's face.

Grey Cloak caught a glimpse of Streak latched onto the back end of the attacking dragon. "It's Streak! He took control of the beast!" He patted Dyphestive on the shoulder.

The brothers looked at each other, eyes filled with surprise.

Grey Cloak poked his brother's broad chest. "You're solid again!"

A barbarian jumped from the rocks above them.

Dyphestive caught the man in midair and slammed him headfirst to the ground. "I am solid again, solid as iron!"

"How's the ankle?"

"I can walk on it. It feels better for some reason." He picked up the battle axe he'd been carrying earlier. "It's not the Iron Sword, but it will do."

A second barbarian charged, steel in hand, through the twisting path in the rocks.

Dyphestive swung his axe into the man's face. "Come on." He stepped over the dead man, holding Grey Cloak up by the waist with one arm and carrying the battle axe in the other. "We're getting out of this death trap."

Black Wolf barred their path. Sword in one hand and battle axe in the other, the black-haired warrior bristled. "The only escape for you is the grave."

33

WITH HIS CLAWS sunk into the top of the tail, Streak assumed full control of the middling dragon's body as if it were his own. *Now all I need to do is defeat the other dragon. Let's try this.*

He snuck in a tail whip that smacked the Risker out of the saddle. The man fell over the arena wall and crashed to the ground. The dragons engaged, their claws raking the scales off one another's chests. Their wings beat furiously.

He's a nasty fighter. Or is it a she? Either way, I'm smarter.

Streak's command of the dragon was flawless. The giant lizards grappled. He used the claws on the tip of the dragon's wing to poke the other dragon in the eye. It bellowed a pain-filled, shrieking roar. Fire shot out of its mouth in the wrong direction.

Let's get a taste of that long neck.

His middling dragon chomped down on the other one. They balled up, their serpentine bodies entwined, busted through arena's top wall, and thrashed across the rocky ground.

Sink those teeth in! Deeper!

His dragon's bite pierced through scale into flesh. Streak could taste dragon blood on his tongue.

Finish him!

The other dragon's muscles gave way. It gave a desperate death call and thrashed fiercely.

I have you now! Crunch!

The dragon's neck snapped. He shook the few remaining moments of life out of it.

That's not the end of it.

His dragon wheeled around and faced off against the two Riskers thrown from their saddles. They were a formidable pair in full black armor and open-faced steel helms with steel wings decorating the sides. They bared their swords and came forward, crouching low.

Streak sent a stream of fire into the closest one. The man scrambled away. He chased him down, pinned the man in the rocks, and covered him in flames. He caught the other Risker charging his backside. He flipped his tail like a whip and hit the man in the chest.

The warrior fell flat on his back. He hopped back to his feet in time to be smashed by the dragon's tail again.

Taste my flames!

In a moment, the Risker was consumed by a stream of dragon fire. He took off running, trying to tear his armor off. He rolled in the snow while frantically trying to pat the flames out. He still burned.

He's done for. Let's find my friends. He set his eyes on the barbarians swarming through the stands and pouring over the arena wall. *But let's turn these guys into kindling first.*

"We don't have to fight, Black Wolf. Look around. Your plan is failing." Dyphestive faced off with him. "Your cause is lost."

Black Wolf spit on the ground. "It's Hercullon who is lost, young fool!" He charged, head low, as quick as a panther.

Steel rang against steel. *Clang!*

Dyphestive parried his opponent's axe. Black Wolf thrust his sword at Dyphestive's gut. He twisted out of reach and pushed Black Wolf away.

"You fight a coward's fight!" Black Wolf moved like a wild beast and attacked with fury. His blades cut through the air in the blink of an eye.

Dyphestive parried both weapons at the same time. He twisted his axe head, pinning Black Wolf's blades, and ripped the axe from the barbarian's hand.

"Clever!" Black Wolf dropped down and launched his foot into Dyphestive's gut.

He doubled over. "Oof."

Black Wolf lifted his sword overhead. "It's over!" He brought it down with two hands. "Vengeance for my son!"

Dyphestive covered his neck with his forearm. The sword bit straight to the bone.

Black Wolf stepped back. "Impossible." Blood dripped from the edge of his blade. "What sort of wizardry is this? Your arm should be crawling on the snow. What manner of man are you?"

"I am Iron Bones!" Dyphestive hurled his axe at Black Wolf.

Black Wolf ducked it. "You're a witch. We burn your kind at the stake." He raised his arms and howled like a wolf. "Brethren, finish them once and for all!"

Dyphestive backed up and shielded Grey Cloak. "They don't quit, do they?"

"It reminds me of someone I know." Grey Cloak called to the sky, "Streak, get us out of here!"

The middling dragon landed on the ground nearby.

Grey Cloak shoved Dyphestive in the back. "Go! Go!"

They climbed into the dragon's saddle.

The dragon's wings beat thunderously. It pushed off the ground into the sky and rose higher.

"How's your arm?" Grey Cloak asked.

"Still attached," Dyphestive remarked.

Without warning, the barbarians took aim. Bowstrings snapped. A volley of arrows sailed toward the dragon. Feathered shafts tore through the dragon's wings and buried themselves between its scales. Another volley came, one after the other. The dragon bucked and roared in midflight.

"It's days like this I miss trips to Thannis," Grey Cloak commented. "Streak, can you get us out of here or not?"

They only made it a hundred feet into the air. The dragon's wings beat furiously. It started to descend.

Dyphestive caught a full look at the township. Many of the buildings were in flames. Smoke filled the sky, and frightened people ran in all directions. The grand dragons glided over rooftops, spitting flames and setting the town on fire.

Dyphestive clenched his fist. "We have to stop this."

Grey Cloak watched with him. "I don't think we can." He looked down. "But we have our own problems. We're falling."

Another volley of arrows sailed into the sky and connected with the dragon.

Thuk! Thuk! Thuk!

The dragon spiraled down toward the arena, where hordes of barbarians waited.

Streak's white eyes turned back to their normal bright

yellow. "This dragon's finished. Prepare yourselves for a crash landing." He peeled away from the dragon's back and took flight. "See you at the bottom, unless the wolves get to you first."

"*OSID-AYAN-UMRA-SHOKRAH-HA*!" Grey Cloak said.

The Figurine of Heroes in his hand started to smoke.

"Hang on to me, brother!" he said as their dragon rushed to meet the ground.

"I'll be fine," Dyphestive said.

The Cloak of Legends fluffed out, lifting Grey Cloak from the dragon's back. He drifted slowly toward the ground.

Streak flew beside him and hovered in the air. He coughed. "What's with all the smoke?"

"I used the figurine." Grey Cloak watched the barbarians gather beneath him.

Dyphestive and the dragon plummeted toward the arena and crashed hard into the rocks. The barbarians kept their eyes on Grey Cloak, pointing at him with their weapons and shouting.

The figurine's smoke thickened, smothering his vision.

Cough, cough. "Man, that stuff is nasty," Streak said. "I can't see a thing."

"Streak, fly down there and give us some cover."

"You got it."

Grey Cloak floated until his toes touched the ground. He was surrounded by inky smoke and coughing. "Dyphestive, are you alive?"

"Never better. I can't say the same for the dragon, but he helped break my fall."

Grey Cloak shushed him. The barbarians were close, grumbling and murmuring. He set the figurine on the ground and stumbled.

"Did you trip over me?" Dyphestive asked.

"I must have."

"Boss!" Streak hollered from above. "Where are you?"

"Where do you think I am?" Grey Cloak heard the flutter of dragon wings.

Streak landed on top of him. "I smoked them out—well, back. But they're waiting for the smoke to clear."

"How many?"

"A score or two, maybe three. We can handle them."

A new form took shape in the inky mist.

"I hope whoever it is, is on our side," Streak stated as the smoke began to clear.

"Me too," Grey Cloak said. "It's been a bad enough day already."

A man appeared in the fading smoke. He had a large head, short brown hair, narrow shoulders, dark, penetrating eyes, and a bookish demeanor. He wore a set of forest-green robes with arcane symbols sewn into the fabric and the hems trimmed in golden layers. His sleeves flopped when he fanned the smoke from his face with his free hand. Tucked underneath his other arm was a leather tome. He eyed the brothers and spoke with an impatient tone. "I take it you're in need of some assistance?"

"Yes," Grey Cloak replied.

"Well, spit it out, or do I have to do all the thinking for you?" the man replied. "If you want help, you have to know what sort of help you need."

"We're surrounded by barbarians," he blurted.

The wind blew more smoke away, and the angry faces of the Wolves from the Rocks began to appear. One of them hurled a spear through the cloud. It whizzed by the newcomer's face, missing him by a nose.

"Ah." The man in robes waved his arm over his head in a half circle. A dome of energy formed around them. "Barbarians, you say. They're going to hate me. Let me ask, how would you like me to dispose of them? Perhaps a tempest that whisks them away."

Grey Cloak and Dyphestive stood up, watching the barbarians attack the dome of energy with vigor. Their eyes were set on the man inside the glowing shell as they screamed, "Slay the wizard!"

"Are you a wizard?" Grey Cloak asked.

"Obviously. But we prefer the term mage or magi where I come from." He leafed through the pages of his leather-bound book. "My name is Fogle Boon, and who might you be?"

"Uh, Grey Cloak. This is my brother, Dyphestive, and my dragon, Streak."

Fogle Boon traced his long finger over the page. "Nice to meet you. But I don't have time to chat. My wife is very demanding, and when she finds out I've been summoned to another world and abandoned my parental duties, well, she'll be very upset. Have you ever met an upset brigand queen?"

"No," they said.

"You don't want too. Ah." He looked at the blood brothers and smiled. "This spell will really screw with their heads. In my experience, most barbarians are all skull and little gray matter." He pushed his hand outward. "Stand back."

Grey Cloak and company backed away.

Fogle Boon's lips moved like a hummingbird's wings while his finger quickly ran down the page. The air inside the dome prickled. The hairs on their arms stood on end.

With a razor-thin smile, Fogle Boon closed the spell

book and held it affectionately to his chest. "Observe your foul and malodorous attackers."

In the wink of an eye, every other barbarian took the shape and form of Fogle Boon the wizard. With savage fury, the unchanged barbarians attacked their own. Sword blades sliced. Axes chopped. Barbarians disguised as wizards rose up and went down. Daggers did permanent damage. Howling men collapsed in tangled piles of limbs. The Wolves from the Rock massacred one another.

Fogle Boon managed a faint giggle. "Why do the work yourself, when they will do it all for you? It's ugly work, but it keeps the blood off my clothing. When I return home, I won't receive a scolding." He faced the much younger men. "I believe we're finished here. Can you return me home now? I don't want to keep my beautiful bride waiting."

Barbarians died. Others fled. The Wolves from the Rocks headed for the hills whence they came.

"Er, I'd imagine you'll return soon. The summoning doesn't normally last very long," Grey Cloak offered.

Fogle Boon returned a bored look. He searched the sky. "What is the name of this place?"

"Ice Vale," replied Dyphestive.

"No, it's Gapoli. At least the world is. And what world are you from?"

Fogle sighed and started to speak, but his voice was drowned out by the roar of grand dragons. Commander

Shaw, Dirklen, Magnolia, and their dragons landed on the top wall of the arena. Their glares fixed on the heroes.

35

"Friends of yours?" Fogle Boon asked. He squinted. "The two blonds appear familiar."

Even though they were far away, they all had keen eyesight, and through the energy dome that slightly obscured their vision, Grey Cloak and Magnolia met eyes.

He turned away. "Don't look at them."

"Why? Will they turn us to stone?" Fogle opened his spell book. "I have an uneasy feeling about that trio, and those dragons are humongous. They'll gobble you whole."

Commander Shaw, Dirklen, and Magnolia rode their dragons down the empty stands. The dragons crushed the bodies of the fallen beneath their paws.

"Fogle, I don't mean to sound impolite, but whatever you are going to do, do it soon." Grey Cloak was out of tricks, and they had nowhere left to run.

Words buzzed out of Fogle's mouth like a swarm of bees. A loud thunderclap boomed overhead. Everyone glanced to the sky. Small black clouds took form over the arena.

Fogle opened and closed his spellbook. Each time, it shrank a size smaller until it fit in the palm of his hand. He put it away inside the sleeve of his robe. "I have to hide it from Jarla. She becomes antsy when I dabble with it." His image started to fade into smoke. "Lads, it's been nice getting out of the tower and tasting some action. It's been a while." He pointed at the sky. "I leave you with this parting gift."

The black clouds pulsed with lightning. Bolts of fire rained down from the sky. Thick cords of bright energy blasted into the three Riskers and their dragons. They spasmed and bucked like mules. Dragon bones radiated inside the skin of the dragons' wings. They roared in pain. Fire from the sky kept coming down. All three dragons and their riders took to the sky and flew away. The black clouds gave chase.

Grey Cloak, Dyphestive, and Streak stood in the stillness of the arena. The energy dome dissipated. Aside from the dead, the barbarians were gone. Black char marks marred the stands. Blood stained the stones. An awful, catastrophic battle had taken place, and somehow they had won.

Clapping echoed from the southern arena tunnel. Tula

appeared. The older elven woman wore a full-length woolen gray coat. She eased down the stairs to the bottom row and looked down on the trio. "Well done." Tula smiled. She sat on the edge of the wall. "I watched the entire event unfold. I can't believe you prevailed, for now."

Grey Cloak picked up the figurine and ambled toward her. He barely had the strength to move. "Thanks for the help."

She shrugged. "I did what you asked. I saw Hercullon to safety."

"And how is he?"

"Safe and breathing. For now."

"Why do you keep saying *for now*?"

Streak jumped up, flew, and landed beside her.

Tula petted his head. "You won the battle, but the war has come."

"What do you mean?"

"Come up and see."

Grey Cloak and Dyphestive made their way into the stands and moved to the top row.

The Ice Vale township burned. The citizens scrambled to put out the flames using carts and sleighs filled with snow.

"They'll get it under control," Grey Cloak said.

"You are shortsighted. The fire isn't the problem. Look in the distance," Tula suggested.

"I see them," Dyphestive said. "A lot of them."

Commander Shaw and his children might have departed, but only temporarily. Beyond the township, more Riskers circled in the snowy sky. Dozens of them. They weren't alone. A wave of soldiers marched toward Ice Vale, cavalry and foot soldiers walking alongside horse-drawn sleighs. It was an invasion.

"I thought we beat them," Grey Cloak said dejectedly. "How will we stop that?"

Tula looked him in the eye. "You can't. You can only save the ones you can. You did that. I'm proud of you." She turned toward Dyphestive. "I'm proud of you both."

"And me?"

"You too, Streak," she said.

Grey Cloak gave her a funny look. "You're being strange." Her kind words struck him as odd, and it made him uncomfortable.

"What are we going to do, Grey?" Dyphestive asked. "There are too many. We can't fight them all."

"Ice Vale is under siege. They would be wise to surrender. It's the only way they can survive. Like me, the three of you need to flee. You can do nothing now. It's over," Tula said. "And the longer you stand planted here, the more likely you'll be captured. Commander Shaw and his children will be looking for you. You might have surprised them once, but you won't surprise them again."

"Don't be so sure about that." Grey Cloak picked up Streak and placed him inside his hood. "Come on, brother, we need to go." He nodded at Tula. "Thanks for the warning. Best to you, Tula." He made his way down the stairs, Dyphestive trailing him.

Tula called after him, "You're going to leave me here, standing in the cold?"

"You can take care of yourself." He moved into the tunnel.

The Iron Sword was propped against the wall. They stopped.

Tula leaned over the tunnel wall. "Did you find my gift?"

Dyphestive picked the sword up and smiled. "Yes!" He looked up at her. "How?"

She shrugged. "I have my ways. So, can I tag along, or are you going to abandon me again?"

"Brother, she should come with us," Dyphestive suggested.

"I concur," Streak said.

Grey Cloak sighed. "Fine."

Tula jumped the wall and landed in the tunnel entrance. "Fantastic," she said. "Follow me."

36

THE TOWNSHIP STREETS were in chaos. People battled fires. Others boarded themselves up in their homes. A great deal of them fled to the cottages and caves in the surrounding countryside. Tula led them straight into the heart of the city.

"Do you mind explaining why we're going into the heart of danger and not away from it?" Grey Cloak asked.

Dragons passed overhead, releasing earsplitting dragon calls.

Skreeeeeeeeeeeee!

Skreeeeeeeeeeeee!

Skreeeeeeeeeeeee!

"That's why," Tula responded as she briskly navigated the streets. "You don't go into the open fields where they can spot you. The smoke and fire conceals us. It's safer."

It made sense, even though Grey Cloak didn't want to admit it. Reluctantly, he followed her, but after turning from one street to another alley, he grabbed her arm and pulled her to a stop. "Enough! Tell us where you're taking us now!"

"I'm looking for a place to hide."

"Burning buildings aren't good places to hide. You'll have to do better than that," he said.

"A very good place to hide," Tula added.

He didn't take his eyes off her. "By leading us in circles. We've been down this road twice now." He grabbed her by the coat and pushed her against the wall. "Explain!"

"Easy, Grey. She's only trying to help," Dyphestive said.

"Are you certain about that?"

"She gave me my sword, didn't she? Why would she do that?"

"Oh, I don't know. Maybe it's so you can stand out like a sore thumb. As if you didn't stand out enough already." Grey Cloak took a breath and loosened his grip. "Pah! I'm not fooling with her anymore. Either come with me or don't."

Dyphestive met Tula's eyes. "Sorry. I'm going with him, but thank you for my sword." He hurried down the road to catch up with his brother. "Bye."

Tula leaned against the wall. "If you don't stay with me, you'll get caught. You can trust me. I swear it."

Grey Cloak waved his arm. "Not listening."

A strong gust of wind blasted down the street, creating icy dust devils. Snow drifts buried their feet, then the harsh wind died down. A quiet moment followed. Grey Cloak flapped the snow from his cloak.

Middling dragons buzzed overhead and blew fire into the buildings. Two of them landed on the opposite ends of the road and set innocent people on fire.

Skreeeeeeeeeee!

Skreeeeeeeeeee!

"We're cut off!" Grey Cloak moved back toward the middle of the street, where he'd left Tula. She dashed into a narrow alley. He pushed Dyphestive from behind. "Go! Go!"

Dyphestive hobbled when he ran. His broad shoulders scraped against the alley walls as he plowed through the wooden crates and knocked over barrels.

They emerged on the next road and ducked underneath the porches.

Dragons flew in low patterns with their bellies and tails scraping rooftops.

Skreeeeeeeeeee!

Skreeeeeeeeeee!

Grey Cloak gave Tula an irritated look. "Where to now?"

She pointed across the street at the opposite alley. "There!"

Grey Cloak spotted a bright-red door. A wooden sign

hanging on chains rattled in the wind. There was no mistaking the storefront. It was Batram's Bartery and Arcania. "We can't get in there!" he shouted above the dragon roars and howling winds.

Two more grand dragons came around the opposing blocks and entered the street. Their bright eyes gleamed like gemstones. Their long necks swung around, revealing their unmistakable riders.

Grey Cloak pushed them back into the alley. "That's Dirklen and Magnolia. Of all Riskers!"

"We need to make a run for it," Tula urged them. "You have to trust me." She caught their doubtful looks. "I'm not waiting. I'm going." She ran.

Grey Cloak peeked around the corner. The twins, Dirklen and Magnolia, watched Tula run across the broad street. Their dragons stalked forward. He knew they could close the gap in an instant.

"Can you run at all?"

Dyphestive offered a hopeful smile. "No, but I can hop like a one-legged frog."

"You really need to work on the timing of your humor." He scooped Dyphestive up in his arms. "Better yet, don't try any humor at all. Thunderbolts, you're heavy."

"What are you doing?"

He crept toward the end of the alley and slipped off his boots using only his feet. "I'm going to make a run for it." Tula already stood at that red door on the other side. It opened, and she went inside. "Hang tight!" His first step slipped on the snow. He gained his footing and took off like a jackrabbit.

"There!" Dirklen hollered.

The red door had opened fully and began to close again. Grey Cloak's legs pumped harder. He stretched his stride. He glanced toward Magnolia and caught her eye. He winked and blew her a kiss at the same time.

I can't help myself.

The dragons galloped at full speed toward his position. Flames shot from their mouths.

He gained speed. The red door was open no more than a crack.

"Hang on!"

"You can't make that jump," Dyphestive said.

The wind whistled in his ears. "We're about to find out." At the foot of the porch, he jumped with his brother in his arms. He cleared five steps, hit the porch running, and busted through the crack in the door. They tumbled to the floor, and the red door closed behind them, muting the deafening dragon roars.

"Welcome!" the throaty boar's-head rug said. "Don't forget to wipe your feet!"

Grey Cloak crawled off of Dyphestive and wiped the snow from his naked feet. "Gladly."

"Ah, that feels good." The rug's corkscrew tail wiggled. "Very good."

Dyphestive lay on the carpet and scratched the boar behind the ears.

"No one's ever done that before," said the boar's head. "Thank you."

Grey Cloak helped his brother to his feet. "Don't get carried away." He took a breath and stared at the front door. Dragons and enemies that wanted to tear him apart were on the other side, but for some reason, he felt safe inside the ancient walls of the arcania. "Never thought I'd be so glad to be here."

Tula stood in front of the glass display cases, examining the contents inside.

The vaulted ceilings were rich in cobwebs, the spiders busy at work crawling along the array of shelving behind the counters. Half-melted candles in their candelabras created puddles of wax on the counters and floors. They saw no sign of Batram.

"It seems you've been here before," Grey Cloak said to Tula.

She shrugged. "Perhaps a time or two."

"Interesting." He moved to the counter that stood taller than eye level. Streak crawled out of his hood onto the counter.

"Mmm, spiders." Streak's tongue flicked out of his mouth and snatched a spider that crawled across the countertop.

Batram appeared out of nowhere and stood upon the

counter. He was in halfling form, hair white and fuzzy, wearing his red-and-white striped coat. He held a rolled scroll in his hand and started hitting Streak on the head with it. "Spit out my little friend, you ferocious beast!"

Streak gulped. "Ferocious? That's a new one."

Batram tipped his head back and sighed. He faced Grey Cloak, bent over, and hit him on the head with the scroll. "You owe me a spider! Young people and pets. They never know how to train them." He turned to Tula, smiled all over, and said pleasantly, "Ah, Zanna Paydark, a pleasant surprise. What brings you here?"

Grey Cloak caught Zanna Paydark giving Batram a cutoff signal with her hand. She dropped her hand quickly when she caught him looking and turned her attention back to the display case.

"You're Zanna Paydark?" Dyphestive asked. He limped over to stand beside his brother and rubbed the wrist that Black Wolf had tried to chop off. It had begun to heal. "That can't be. Zanna Paydark died, seasons ago."

"I didn't realize the three of you haven't met." Bartram rubbed his bushy sideburns. "I assumed you were together when you entered, naturally."

"As I understand it, this is Tula." Grey Cloak glared at her. "So, which is it, Tula or Zanna Paydark? My mother. Who's"—he raised his voice and lifted a finger—"supposed to be dead."

Batram plopped down on the counter. His short legs dangled over the edge. "Oh, this is getting interesting." A white-and-red-striped container appeared in his hands. It contained fluffy white pieces of food that crunched as he ate them.

"Popcorn." Streak joined Batram. "Can I have some? It's been a while."

Batram offered the runt dragon the container. "Yes, help yourself." He suddenly jerked it away. "On second thought, no. You ate my spider."

"Aaaah," Streak said with disappointment.

"Tula, who are you?" Grey Cloak demanded. "My mother, er, Zanna Paydark is dead. You're an imposter."

Zanna tucked her hair behind her ear and sighed. "Why would anyone impersonate Zanna Paydark?"

"You're dodging the question." His voice became bitter. "Who are you?"

She faced him and stared into his eyes. "Who do you think I am?"

There was no mistaking the strong resemblance. Though her hair was messy, her angular elven features were the same. The gray in her eyes was a perfect match to his.

Dyphestive leaned over Grey Cloak's shoulder. "You have to admit she looks a lot like you."

"Perhaps she's a chameleon," he stated.

"Hah! I'm no such thing. Chameleons are extremely rare, and I killed the last one in our vicinity."

Streak snuck behind Batram and nipped a big bite of popcorn.

"Hey!" Batram swatted at him with his scroll. "Go away, spider-eating pest!" He cleared his throat. "Perhaps I can clear matters up and give the young Grey Cloak some reassurance. This is indeed Zanna Paydark. I can vouch for that. She's been a customer in the bartery for many years."

Grey Cloak crossed his arms. "If that's the case, and you're indeed my mother, then what's my real name?"

"It certainly isn't Grey Cloak," she scoffed. "I'd never give a child of mine such a silly name."

He frowned. "It's not silly."

"You named yourself after a garment."

"Why does everyone say that?"

Zanna's stern expression softened. She came closer to him and placed her hands on his shoulders. "Your name is Dindae. It means *my little shadow*." Her words rang true.

His eyes began to water. He broke away from her. "It can't be. My mother is dead."

"I'm not dead. At least, not in the sense most people would believe it. There is a lot you don't know and need to understand. I believe now is an opportune time to explain it."

Grey Cloak clenched his jaw. He was angry when he should be happy. She infuriated him.

Dyphestive tapped Zanna on the shoulder. "I believe you, but I have a question. Can you tell me what happened to my father? Is he alive too?"

The room quieted. Only Batram's obnoxious crunching could be heard.

"The less you know, the better," she said.

"Oh yes, here we go. Another dodge," Grey Cloak said.

"Hush. I want to know the truth," Dyphestive insisted.

Zanna reached up and touched his face. "And you deserve it. Your father is a very dear friend of mine—a Sky Rider, the same as me." She stood before him and offered a solemn look. "Olgstern Stronghair is alive, but he would be better off dead."

38

___

GREY CLOAK DIDN'T TALK, but he listened to every word his alleged mother said. He stood with his back to the wall, leaning against it with his arms crossed and frowning as Zanna Paydark continued to spin her story while the others hung on her every word.

"It all came down to the Day of Betrayal," Zanna solemnly said. "The Sky Riders were at full strength, more than equipped to take the monster dragon down. Led by your father, Olgstern, we flew to Dark Mountain fully prepared to launch our attack." She paced with her arms crossed and spoke with a serious look on her face. "I'll never forget the day—over one hundred Sky Riders flying in formation with dragon wings shining against the sun. One single focus. One single mind. Or so we thought.

"At that time, we'd come to understand the nature of Black Frost's rise to power. We knew that he had tapped the vein of another world and that was where he drew his power. What we didn't know was how to stop it or close the portal, but the Sky Riders agreed, one step at a time. We needed to destroy Black Frost and close the portal after." She leaned on the display case and fixed her eyes on the objects that gleamed inside the glass.

"Unfortunately, he was one step ahead of us. We arrived at Dark Mountain with superior numbers, outmatching the Riskers three to one. It should have been an easy victory. It would prove to be anything but. As we circled the temple, remaining airborne, we urged Black Frost to surrender. Instead, he stood his ground in sheer defiance and gave us a warning." Her face darkened. "'Join me or die.'"

She continued with a haunted look in her eyes. "We laughed. Can you believe it? From our lofty heights, we actually sniggered, never realizing the full extent of our danger. We were so arrogant, so full of pride, so angry, but we were blinded. We had vengeance in our eyes. You see, Black Frost killed your father, Grey Cloak, and your mother, Dyphestive. And that wasn't all. He weakened the other Sky Riders as well with his brazen attack. Little did we know that he was setting us up for the Great Fall."

"Olgstern Stronghair ordered the attack. We began our descent in attack formation. The Riskers and their dragons stood their ground, guarding Black Frost on the top of the temple. I saw his eyes and the spark of deceit within—a predator about to devour his prey. I'll never forget the moment, the feeling of my stomach sinking into my toes." She hung her head. "We were attacked by our very own."

Batram had created two more small buckets of popcorn and shared them with Streak and Dyphestive. They all stuffed the fluffy white kernels in their mouths, crunching loudly.

"That sucks." Streak buried his nose in the bucket of food. "What happened?" He rolled onto his back, picked up the bucket, and dumped its remaining contents into his wide-open mouth. "Mmm, that's good."

Zanna didn't show any irritation in her creaseless forehead. "Two-thirds of the Sky Riders turned on their kind. They flew in the formation's back ranks and attacked everyone before them. Their arrows and javelins intended for the Riskers struck against their own men. The Riskers guarding the temple attacked. We were caught off guard, hemmed in by our very own, and outnumbered.

"Black Frost only added salt to the wound. He was four times bigger than any other dragon. His scorching flames consumed grand dragons whole. In the flick of a lash, we were lost. Honorable Sky Riders perished that day. Others succumbed to evil. We only had one last play to make."

Grey Cloak's heart beat in his ears. Her words drew him in as if he were reliving all she said.

"Olgstern and I agreed. We told Justus and the others to

flee. The battle was lost. We stayed behind and drew the enemy's fire," Zanna continued. "I had no doubt that Black Frost's power came from deep within the temple. That was why he guarded it so heavily. Determined to unravel his secret, we drove our dragons into the heart of evil, summoning as much of our shields as we could to protect us. I had a ruse. Olgstern crashed onto the top level, where smoke and flames already billowed. I scattered more smoke in all directions using vials, much like you do." She gave Streak an approving look. "Because it's always prudent to have a backup plan.

"Taking advantage of the confusion, using the cover of smoke and darkness, we navigated our way into the bowels of the temple and descended deep into its depths. At the bottom, we traced the energy source that fed him, where we confirmed he was draining the vibrant life force of another world. Our goal was simple—cut off the source and destroy the portal—but we had no idea how. We followed the signs and wandered into the chamber, where we saw an open portal and glimpsed another world. It was a beautiful place, with marvelous vegetation and fields of wonder, but the colorful landscapes were turning gray. The eye of the portal burned like a great lantern, but there was no way to shut it." She sighed. "We crept closer. My skin felt pricked by a thousand needles. Tiles covering pressure plates gave way. We were consumed by gas and turned into solid stone."

Grey Cloak applauded slowly. "Magnificent story, but if you were turned to stone, how did you wind up here?"

Zanna smirked. "That story is a lot more complicated."

39

Dᴙᴩʜᴇsᴛɪᴠᴇ ʀᴇsᴛᴇᴅ his head in his hands. "So, my father is a statue?"

"Take heart, Festive. There is hope for him, thanks to you and Grey Cloak. I'm very proud of you both, and no doubt your father will be too."

Grey Cloak stood. "Explain how it is you came to be here and how he's stuck there."

"The less you know, the better. It's risky enough that we've been forced into contact. I tried to avoid it," she said.

"Obviously," Grey Cloak stated.

"I know this is difficult, but show some respect. I am your mother."

He shook his head. "I don't know you."

"Festive, is he always hardheaded?" she asked.

"It can be an issue."

Zanna Paydark took off her coat and set it down on the countertop. "Batram, I'm going to need some new clothing." Her old garments were moth-eaten and frayed. "See what you can find me while I talk to the children."

Batram pulled a handkerchief out of his front pocket and wiped his hands. "I imagine I'll find something. It's been good to see you after all these years. I've missed your visits." He glanced at Grey Cloak. "His, not so much. He's made out like a bandit and still owes me for the cloak."

Grey Cloak tightened his cloak around his body. "No, I don't."

Batram grew into his monstrous form, standing over ten feet tall with a bug-eyed face and eight insect arms. He leaned over the counter and said in a demonic voice, "Yes, you do!" He took Zanna Paydark's cloak, bowed to her, turned, and walked away.

"I wouldn't upset Batram. He's an ally we desperately need," Zanna said. "I've spent decades building a strong relationship with him. I'd hate for you to spoil it." She eyed the Cloak of Legends. "As you can see, it has benefitted you as well."

"What do you mean?" he asked.

"I left the Cloak of Legends for you. It used to be mine, but I gave it to Batram. I told him to let you have it if you ever walked in here one day."

Grey Cloak scoffed. "You're only saying that."

She gave him a nonchalant look. "You can ask him if you like."

"I don't think I could take his word any more than I would take yours."

"Cut her some slack, boss," Streak stated. "I would never talk to my mother like that. And I'd be thrilled if I ever even met her."

"Why is everyone against me? I'm not the one who avoided my children for decades. She abandoned me."

"No, I didn't. Black Frost captured us after he killed your father, Jerrik. He was a wizard of the Watch, a very kind man. He is the one who discovered Black Frost's plan." She couldn't hide her guilt. "He's the one who opened the portal. He tried to close it again, but Black Frost betrayed him."

Grey Cloak gave her a haughty look. "My, don't you spin a fine tale? Let me guess. Dyphestive's mother spins yarn into gold."

Zanna slapped his face. "Don't speak ill of the dead. Like it or not, I'm your mother. Jerrik was your father, and Festive's father is made of stone. It hurts. I have to live with it. I protected you from that. Festive's mother, Careena, was my best friend, a vision of grace and kindness, and I saw her destroyed." She poked him in the chest. "Now you know. Now you can live with that!"

Grey Cloak rubbed his sore cheek. "Sorry." He smirked. "But it's been a long day."

"It's been a long lifetime." Zanna took a deep breath. "But thanks to you two, believe it or not, we can put an end to this madness." She showed a space between her thumb and finger. "We are this close. Will you listen or not?"

"I'm all earholes," Streak said.

Dyphestive pushed himself up on one leg. Popcorn rolled off his chest onto the floor. He stooped down and offered Zanna a sheepish smile. "Can I have a hug?"

Zanna's eyes teared up. She opened her arms. "Of course you can."

Grey Cloak's throat tightened. He swallowed the lump building inside it. In his heart of hearts, he knew the truth, that the woman standing before him was his mother, Zanna Paydark. She beckoned him over with her hand. He moved in, and they all embraced.

Dyphestive sobbed. His rumblings shook them like leaves.

"Let me get in on this." Streak wormed himself into the action. "Ah, that feels nice."

Zanna broke away and wiped her eyes. She sniffed. "Whew, I haven't felt anything in a long time. It's good to feel again." She cupped Grey Cloak's face in her warm palms. "When I saw you in the dungeon, I thought it was a dream. I thought about you every day. Believe me when I say it pained me not to reveal myself until it became absolutely essential."

"I don't understand," Grey Cloak said.

"You should. You will, better than anyone. I don't mean to be mysterious, but the less you know, the better. Otherwise it could alter how I arrived here," she said.

Dyphestive snapped his fingers with a loud pop. "You went through the Time Mural, too, didn't you?"

Zanna didn't say, but Grey Cloak saw in her eyes that she had. "But how?"

"As I've stated. It's complicated. If I say, it could have a catastrophic effect on the past, present, and future." Zanna took Streak out of Grey Cloak's arms, cradled him, and stroked him like a cat. "Revealing myself to you is dangerous enough, but at this junction, it's necessary."

"So, you were sent to find us?" Grey Cloak asked. His thoughts spun like a miller's wheel. "What for?"

"To finish your training. We can't afford to let your talents go to waste anymore."

40

STILL IN MONSTROUS FORM, Batram moseyed toward them from the long corridor behind the counter. He stood tall between the shelves and drawers that ranged from as large as coffins at the bottom to small enough to hold a thimble at the top. He put a set of neatly folded clothing on the counter. "I think you'll find these to your liking, Zanna." He crossed his four upper arms and pushed the garb toward her. "Please, try them on."

Zanna took the clothing and smiled. "I'll be right back." She pulled back the violet curtain stretched over the corner of the room, entered, and closed it.

The brothers shared a curious look.

"She'll probably be a while." Batram drummed his fingers on the glass case. "While you're waiting, why don't you take a look at some new items I've acquired?" He reached below and produced a brass lantern. "This will summon an arguably helpful spirit if you rub it."

"No, I have something like that." Grey Cloak stared into the case, and his brother joined him.

An array of necklaces, bracelets, and rings sparkled like stars. Fine weaponry was on full display, including axes, swords, and daggers of all sorts, as were brooches and earrings, gauntlets, bracers, lanterns, candles, stacks of rolled-up scrolls, shined boots, and soft leather ones.

Grey Cloak yawned. "I'm so tired, I can't think."

"Perhaps something for the larger gentleman, then." Batram revealed a large warrior's helm fashioned like a dragon's skull. He ran his spidery fingers over the polished steel surface. "It has very unique powers."

"Can it make me fly?" Dyphestive asked.

"No."

"Ah, well, no thanks, then."

"Ahem." Zanna stepped out from behind the curtain. Her messy hair was tied back in a ponytail. She wore a long-sleeved black jerkin tied off in a knot above her belly. A storm-gray sash dressed her hips, and her fitting trousers were pitch-black. The ink-colored boots she donned came above her ankles and were cuffed at the top.

Batram nodded. "A good fit."

"A very good fit," Dyphestive commented with big eyes.

Grey Cloak slapped him in the chest.

"What?" Dyphestive shrugged. "I need new clothing too. Can I get something in black?"

"Thanks for the clothing, Batram. I'm going to need some weapons to match." She pointed at the case to a pair of finely crafted daggers with silver handles. "I'll take those, that. I'll need some healing salve, hmmm... I like that short sword, and ..."

Batram pulled out the items she asked for.

Zanna strapped the silver daggers on her thighs. She slung the short sword over her shoulder.

"Here, I'll give you the assortment you usually require." Batram added small potion vials, jars, and scrolls to a large leather pouch. "Take it and take no more." He gave her an irritated look.

She hung the pack on her shoulder. "Thank you. You always know what a girl needs." She glanced down at Dyphestive's foot. "Can you walk?"

"I can walk, sort of." Dyphestive's ankle was crooked and angled away from his body. "Mad Wolf broke it."

Zanna squatted down. "It's not broken. It's bent. Your father had the same problem."

Dyphestive gave her a curious look. "What are you saying? It's made of metal?"

"Either that or something like it. It's your gift as a natural. One of them anyway." Zanna patted the counter-top. "Climb up here."

"Pardon?" Batram asked.

"The barbarian bent Festive's bones. I need you to bend them back, Batram. You're the only one strong enough to do it," she said.

Batram tapped his chin. "True, but that must have been one strong barbarian."

"When a berserker is enraged, he can bend steel like rope," Zanna said.

"I can bend steel," said Dyphestive. "Let me try it."

"Are you mad? Let Batram do it," Grey Cloak suggested.

It was too late. Dyphestive had already pulled his foot into his lap and grabbed ahold of it. He started to twist. "Huh, I can feel where it's out of place. Urk!" The ankle popped.

Grey Cloak's stomach turned upside down. "I think I'm going to be sick."

Dyphestive gave a proud look. "Hmm, it wasn't bent, only dislocated." He rolled his ankle in small circles. "Did you hear it pop into place?"

"How could we miss it?" Grey Cloak pinched his nose. "Batram, can you get him some new boots? His feet stink."

Zanna giggled.

Batram moved back into the aisles and started opening drawers. "I'll find something. Something for everybody." He whistled a cheerful song.

"Well, Mother, as long as you're waiting, what can you fill us in on? Can you tell me about this cloak? Or is that another big secret?"

Zanna smiled. "I don't see the harm in that. Your father, Jerrik, and I stole it." She walked over to him and smoothed the fabric over his shoulders. "This was before I became a Sky Rider, back when I ran as wild as the wind and worked for the Wizard Watch."

41

"So, you were a thief?" Grey Cloak asked.

"I prefer adventurer or opportunist." Zanna wore a playful look on her face, like she was reliving a wonderful childhood. "It took me a long time to commit to becoming a Sky Rider. I enjoyed myself, but during an encounter with Olgstern, I eventually changed my mind. Jerrik and I decided it was for the best, but it wasn't easy."

Grey Cloak frowned. "I know what you mean. Dyphestive and I were hoping to live our lives on our own terms until Dalsay roped us into this. I can't say I regret it, but we haven't had much of a chance to enjoy our youth. If we weren't shoveling dragon dung in the kennels, we were breaking our backs on Rhonna's farm. Once we were clear of that, we were on the run again."

"I enjoyed it, well, the work on the farm, that is." Dyphestive slid down off the counter. "And some other things too. Think of all the friends we've made."

"And all the friends who've died too. But we're going to save them all," Grey Cloak said.

Zanna placed her hands on his shoulders and petted the fabric of the cloak. "I miss this fine garment. It's a creation from a guild of wizards and thieves in Monarch City. They used it to rob the castle treasuries that were guarded by dragons, and it has many clever powers, which I'm sure you're familiar with."

Grey Cloak lifted his brows up and down. "Really? And what powers did you use?"

"Clever." She smiled at her son. "You want to know the powers I've used that perhaps you haven't. The truth is, I'm not sure that I've experienced them all because the cloak has a mind of its own. Of course, I don't mind sharing a few, but you mentioned one already. We've seen you fall like a feather and absorb the enemy's blows. It can protect you from dragon fire and lets you breathe underwater. Not to mention the plethora of pockets that you can pour gold into."

She'd named all of the abilities that he knew, but he had a feeling she was holding back. "And?"

"And you're a natural. You don't need it. I saw what you did when you fought against the barbarians. They covered you up like mud, but you used wizardry to shed them like a dog sheds water." Zanna poked him in the chest. "That was impressive. Those are the powers you need to focus on. Those are the powers I'll teach."

Grey Cloak tilted his head to one side. "The Sky Riders in Hidemark told me how to use my magic. What else is there to learn?"

"Plenty. Tell me, how long did you learn with them?"

"Not long," he said.

"I never learned anything from them at all," injected Dyphestive. "I only learned from the Doom Riders."

"We'll work on that too. Both of you need to hone your skills. You have plenty of ability and are gifted, even for naturals, but if you aren't at the top of your game, you'll never defeat Black Frost."

Batram returned and dropped two sets of clothing on the counter. "Suit up, boys." He set a pair of black-dyed leather bracers on the table. "I think you'll like those, Zanna. They're your style."

"Thank you." She put the bracers on. Protruding from the tops were the handles of small knives sheathed in the leather. "You can never have too many knives in a scrap."

"Don't you have to pay or trade something for all that?" Grey Cloak asked. "He always makes me pay."

"Zanna has a large line of credit," said Batram. He patted Grey Cloak on the head. "Perhaps one day you'll have one too." He pointed at the clothes on the counter. "That will be thirteen gold pieces."

"What?" He reached into his pocket and handed over the gold chips. "Here."

Batram leaned on his counter. "Look, Zanna, I've enjoyed your company immensely, but you know the rules. You can't hide in the bartery forever. I have other customers to attend to."

"I understand. Get dressed, boys. It's time to go." She offered her hand to Batram, and he shook it with his fuzzy spider legs. "Thank you, old friend."

"Do you mean to tell me we're going right back out into that hornet's nest?" Grey Cloak asked.

"You're rested enough, aren't you?" she asked.

"Yes, but—"

"Do you want me to hold your hand?"

"No," he whined. Grey Cloak got a firm grip on the Rod of Weapons and headed toward the door. "Fine, if we need to do this, we need to do this. I'm ready."

"Wait for me." Dyphestive finished donning the same sort of garb—a sheepskin vest and buckskin trousers—that he typically wore. "I was hoping for something in black." He tugged on his mountain boots. "Ah, but these feel good."

Zanna moved in front of them. "Listen to me. This is vitally important. When we abandon this haven, we need to lie low. We're not going to try saving those who have been lost. We have to avoid them altogether. We are going to hide, and train, until you both return to the time where you last left. That is the only way."

"We can't stand around and do nothing," Grey Cloak said.

Dyphestive stepped forward with his sword. "I agree. If we can save our friends now, we need to do it."

Zanna shook her head. "No! Don't be so hardheaded. You'll ruin everything!" She lowered her voice. "Boys, you are going to have to trust me. It's the only way."

Something about her words bothered Grey Cloak, but he kept his thoughts to himself. "I'm not so sure about that."

They moved toward the door and waved goodbye to Batram.

"Hurry back!" the boar's-head carpet said.

The red door opened wide. An unseen force sent them hurtling out of the store and into the street.

42

GREY CLOAK SPIT the dust from his mouth. He landed face-first on a dusty road and found himself underneath a blanket of warm sunlight. He sat himself up using his hands. The sky was as blue as a robin's egg, and the clouds were white and puffy. Birdsong could be heard among the rumbling of wagon wheels.

"Make way!" a man shouted.

Dyphestive and Zanna scrambled to one side of the road, and Grey Cloak rolled to the other. He braced himself against the foot of the stairs that led up to the porch of a country storefront.

A rickety wagon pulled by a single horse rumbled by. The man driving the wagon wore a big straw hat and had a long-stem corncob pipe in his mouth. He lifted his cap and waved it as he rolled by.

Across the road, Dyphestive's eyes were as big as saucers, and he had a perplexed look on his face. Zanna stood and started dusting herself off. Behind her was Batram's Bartery and Arcania. The ancient structure stood cramped between two buildings, and it faded away in the sun, leaving an empty alley behind it.

"Huh." That was the last thing Grey Cloak had expected, and he put out the fire that burned on the end of the Rod of Weapons.

Behind him, people gawked as they walked along the porch. A young lady, dressed in common garb, hurried down the stairs and offered her hand. "Let me help. Are you hurt?"

He politely took her hand. "I'm well, thank you."

The pie-faced younger woman had big freckles and a small gap between her front teeth. She started brushing the dust off his cloak. "Do you need help up the stairs? Did you fall? I see you're using a cane. I can help you," she said sincerely.

"Cane? How old do you think I am?" he asked.

She became pushy. "Don't be ashamed. We have a special place for cripples. Did you get lost?"

Grey Cloak planted his finger over her lips. "I'll give a piece of silver if you tell me where I am and quickly go away. Agreed?"

She nodded. A silver coin appeared between his thumb

and finger. She gasped. He removed his finger from her lips.

She caught her breath as if she'd been held underwater for minutes and blurted out, "Portham. You're in Portham."

Grey Cloak flipped the coin high. She caught it with two hands and ran like the devil without looking back.

"Portham." Dyphestive scratched his head. "I thought it looked familiar."

"Batram couldn't have left us in a better place," Zanna said. "The people are warm, friendly, and keep to themselves." She studied the group. "But we do stand out a bit. We might need to dress down a tad." She gave Dyphestive the most concerned look. "Because there won't be a lot of people walking around with six-foot-long claymores."

"Well, look at you. You're dressed like a giant black cat," Grey Cloak said.

"Clever, I like it." She patted them on the back. "Don't worry, I'll dress it down. In the meantime, how about I buy you both something to eat? It's time to talk strategy."

Portham was the farthest city in the west of the Westerlund territory and north of Havenstock, where Grey Cloak and Dyphestive had lived with Rhonna for years. They had both spent time on the trails between Portham and Havenstock, picking up loads of supplies for the farms. The citizens of the vast farming community were hardworking and easygoing. True to Zanna's word, they kept about their own business but were more than willing to help. So long as they weren't lazy, or a thief, people were always welcome in Portham.

They stopped in a general goods shop and picked out some gear. Dyphestive bought a big straw hat and some burlap to wrap his sword. Zanna bought a cotton shawl sewn with a pattern of dull colors that covered most of her chest and shoulders. Grey Cloak didn't buy anything, as the Cloak of Legends appeared common enough.

Similar to most cities in Gapoli, Portham was a network of well-built wood, log, and stone structures, but the roads were made of dirt, not paving stones, and everywhere they went, it smelled like straw and livestock. It wasn't without its charms, as there were bountiful gardens one could stroll through, and bridges that arched over fishponds.

The tavern they entered smelled like meat, potatoes, and smoking tobacco. It wasn't very crowded. Dyphestive's stomach grumbled so loud it scared an old woman.

She banged her cane on the floor. "Someone get this boy something to eat." She offered him a toothy smile. "He's famished."

Once they were seated, the servant girl took their order and hurried away.

Zanna leaned back on her chair until she hit the wall. "Relax, boys. We can breathe easy for now. We will eat, plan, and enjoy ourselves."

Grey Cloak rested the rod against the wall in a spot where only he could reach it. He knew the people of

Portham, but he wasn't about to let his guard down either. He put his elbows on the table and hunkered down. After the fight in Ice Vale, he was still drained. "All right, Mother, here we are. What's your *plan*? I'm curious to see if it coordinates with mine."

Streak popped his head out of Grey Cloak's hood. He licked the air with his tongue. "Mmmm... I smell good food. Did you order me something?"

"Of course. Now get back inside the hood. Dragons, big and small, can spook these people."

An imposing man entered the tavern with his sword resting on his shoulder. Grey Cloak crouched out of sight.

"What is it?" Dyphestive followed Grey Cloak's eyes and started to turn.

"Be still!" Grey Cloak whispered.

Dyphestive froze. "Why? Who is it?"

"It's Sash, the leader of the Scourge."

43

THERE WAS no mistaking the short, prickly-haired, fish-eyed leader of the Scourge. He strolled in with an air of confidence, and the patrons scooted their chairs out of his path. Sash wore scale mail, and black ribbons hung from his elbows, waist, and knees. He made his way to the bar, leaned on the counter, and ordered a jug of wine.

Grey Cloak could feel the man's eyes scanning the room as his heart beat in his throat. Under his breath, he said, "Out of all the places, how does he of all people wind up here?"

Dyphestive pulled his straw hat down over his eyes and stooped over the table. "Are you sure it's him?"

"Is a fish fish-eyed?"

"I don't know this man. Should I?" Zanna asked casually.

The waitress returned with plates of food and set them down on the table. Grey Cloak was able to peek around the woman. Sash sucked on a jug of wine and turned his back to them.

Grey Cloak answered Zanna. "He's the leader of the Scourge. Our paths crossed more than once when we joined Talon. They hunted dragon charms the same as we did, and they tried to kill us."

"Remember we're in the past. Have they met you yet?" she asked.

He nodded. "Assuming Hercullon spoke truthfully about Black Frost wiping out the Sky Riders on Gunder Island, yes, we've met. I have no doubt he remembers our faces, and I'm certain he's not alone."

"There's more?" she said.

"I hope not, but most likely, yes."

"What do you think they're doing here?" Dyphestive asked.

Grey Cloak shrugged. "I can only guess that they got wind of some dragon charms in the area. It might serve the greater good to take them out now before they cause more trouble." He narrowed his eyes on Sash. "We can handle them. And they wouldn't know what hit them."

"Agreed," Dyphestive said with a mouthful of food. "We've come a long way. We were practically children then."

"You'll do no such thing," Zanna warned. She started

picking at her food with a fork. "Let the inevitable happen. Lay low, eat, and move on."

"No disrespect, Mother, but you aren't in charge. With that said, I'm willing to heed your advice and listen to what you have in store for us." He took a drink of honey milk served in a carved wooden mug. "I've always loved this swill. Rhonna would rarely buy it for us though. When she did, it was a treat."

"This Rhonna sounds like a fine person," Zanna said.

"She was the mother we never had," Grey Cloak retorted. "No offense. She wasn't a joy to be with."

"I miss Rhonna. Maybe we can go see her," Dyphestive suggested.

Zanna rolled her eyes. "No one is going to see anyone. We have to be discreet and prepare ourselves for the war ahead. We need to exercise patience."

Grey Cloak started into his bowl of stew. "Do you mean to tell me we're going to wait near a decade of seasons before we make contact again?"

"Yes." Zanna nibbled on a hot roll. "There's no other way."

"There has to be another way. After all, we're here. Now. Why don't we try to take out Black Frost?" he suggested.

"That's hardly feasible. Even in his earlier state, Black Frost is too strong. And we don't yet know how to kill him," Zanna said. "Think about it. He destroyed the Sky Riders.

All who were left. It will take an army to defeat him, a massive one. In the future, that is what we build."

Grey Cloak noticed Sash's gaze swing his way, and he ducked out of view. "I better put my hood on. Ol' Fish-eyes appears restless."

Streak crawled out of his hood and onto his lap.

"Better." He put the hood up and shielded his eyes. "Continuing. Since you know where his source of power is, why don't we sneak in there now and destroy it? Think about it. He recently defeated the last of the Sky Riders. His guard will be lowered, and he won't see it coming." He looked for a sign of encouragement from Dyphestive. "We could even free your father at the same time. Black Frost will lose his power and, I don't know, die eventually or be severely weakened."

Zanna chewed on the end of her thumbnail. "I like the idea, but it would be a suicide mission. Even if we cut off his power source, we wouldn't make it out alive. I'm willing to die for our cause, but I'd need greater assurance as to the outcome. And I didn't come back to find you so you could alter my plan. We've decided that waiting it out is the best course of action."

"We who?" Grey Cloak asked.

"Again—"

"I know, the less we know, the better." Grey Cloak sighed. His instincts told him now would be the perfect moment to strike. Perhaps he was getting ahead of himself. He stirred his spoon in his food. "Let's finish this and go."

Zanna reached over and touched his arm. "It's a good plan, but the war is won with patience."

Dyphestive nodded. "I like it, too, and I want to free my father."

"I do too," Zanna assured him.

Grey Cloak picked at his meal as the conversation came to a complete stop. Once everyone finished, he wiped his mouth on his napkin. Sash was slouched over the bar, not talking to anyone. His sword rested across his lap, and he drank heavily.

"It appears now is an opportune time to slip out of here." Grey Cloak tucked Streak underneath his arm and pushed back his chair. "Let's go."

A huge musclebound man filled the tavern's doorway.

"Zooks. It's Bull."

44

WITH BULL LEADING THE WAY, more members of the Scourge filed in, one after the other. Bull was the largest of them, as big as Dyphestive if not bigger. He was as bald as an egg, ugly, and scarred, with lazy eyes. The club in his grip was big enough for two men to carry.

"Interesting bunch of rogues." Zanna wore a playful smile. "Tell me about your friends."

"They aren't friends," Grey Cloak said. "The big one is Bull. He's every bit as dumb as he looks. The woman with green hair is Katrina. She's second-in-command. The little ferret-faced woman with the wolf-fur cloak is Squirrel. The tall swordsman is Hawk, and the scrawny one with the gash on his face and more tattoos than skin on his arms is Honzur—a wizard. Obviously."

"A fetching bunch."

The members of the Scourge one and all bumped forearms with Sash. Their aggressive manners took over the place.

"Don't anyone be alarmed!" Sash said in a throaty voice. He offered up his hands in a sign of peace. "We are here to celebrate! It's been a good day!" He slapped his hand on the top of the bar. "Barkeep, give my friends here all they can drink. A round for present company."

"Hear! Hear!" said a heavyset man sitting in the corner by himself.

"We need to go before this gets out of hand," Grey Cloak said.

Zanna agreed. She hailed the waitress with a nod. "Is there another way out of here?"

"Yes, there's a back door, but the owner doesn't like to see patrons back in his kitchen," the spry little waitress said. "Why don't you stay and have a free drink? The loud one is buying, and we don't get this sort of excitement very often. The owner is even sending word out for a band."

"Here." Zanna paid the young lady. "We don't want anything, as we have someplace to be."

The waitress took the coins and dropped them in the pocket of her apron. "Thank you. If you'll excuse me, I have a lot of work ahead of me."

"Maybe we should split up. If we leave at the same time, it's certain to draw attention," Zanna suggested. "I'll go out the back. After that, the two of you slip out one at a time. Be subtle and take whatever exit is available."

"Brilliant," Grey Cloak muttered. "Go with haste. We'll watch your back."

Zanna eased out of her chair and pulled her shawl tight over her shoulders as she spotted a gap between the bar and the back wall that led into the galley. Head down, she shuffled toward the exit.

With his back to the bar, Sash rolled toward her. He stuck his sword in the wall, barring the gap and blocking her path in a single fluid move. "I've had my eye on you since the moment I walked in." He wiggled his head as he said it. "What's your name, gorgeous?"

Zanna looked Sash in the face. "My name is Tula. And you have a good eye and a sword skill to match."

"Tula. I like it. Why don't you join me for a drink? You see, I've been on a dangerous adventure." He glanced over his shoulder at the others in his group. "And I could use some new company."

"Flattery will get you nowhere," Zanna said politely. She tapped the blade of his sword with her fingernail as she studied his smile full of tobacco-stained teeth. It wasn't the first time she'd dealt with his type. "Why don't you give me a moment to relieve myself, and I'll be back." She placed her hand on his shoulder and squeezed. "Brawn. I like it." She looked at Bull. "But that one is brawnier."

"Him?" Sash chuckled and toyed with her hair. "He couldn't handle a clever woman like you. You aren't from Portham, are you?"

"Passing through with family. Heading north, back home to Kenna."

"Kenna? A country elf. I like that even better." He looked her up and down. "Hmmm... you're packing some interesting merchandise. Why do I get the feeling that you aren't some innocent country elf, eh?"

"Obviously, I'm more than meets the eye. If you'll excuse me, I really have to go. Lady business."

Sash touched his chest and bowed. He pulled his sword free. "I'll let you go, but don't disappoint me. I wouldn't like that."

Zanna returned a winsome smile. "Don't worry, I'll return shortly." She kissed the grizzly hairs on his cheek. "Tah-tah."

Sash leaned over the bar, ogling her as she went into the kitchen. He howled like a dog. "Woo!" He slapped the bar and snatched up a jug. "I think I'm in love!"

"What was that?" Grey Cloak's neck turned red.

Dyphestive replied, "What was what? I can't look, remember?"

"She kissed the cretin."

"On the lips?"

"No, on the cheek, but still, he's a filthy hound." The sight of his mother flirting with Sash stirred feelings he couldn't comprehend. "That was disgusting. Streak, I'm going to walk you to the bar. You go after her and be discreet. We don't need the cooks screaming their heads off because they think there's a giant rat in the kitchen."

"Rat? I'm not a rat," Streak said. "I resent that."

"After that, I'll slip out." He tapped the rod on the plank floor. "Pretending to be an old man. They're getting drunk. I should fool them. Be patient, brother. Once they're soused, try to creep out, front or back. I'll be watching."

Dyphestive straightened his straw hat. "Will do."

Grey Cloak dropped Streak off through the gap in the bar, and the dragon scurried underneath the swinging kitchen doors and into the back. Using the Rod of Weapons like a cane, head down and trembling noticeably, he ambled toward the front exit.

Bull stepped into his path. "Say, old one, where are you going? We're celebrating." He shoved a mug of ale at Grey Cloak. "Drink."

"As you wish, young warrior. I will drink, but I hope my leprosy won't bother you. It's not contagious."

"Huh!" Bull's eyes grew, and he jerked back his drink. He sulked away, saying, "Get out of here, rotten flesh."

Grey Cloak sniggered as he exited through the door. "That was all too easy." He moved to a spot on the porch where he could look through the window.

Dyphestive sat alone at his table. The Scourge weren't paying him any mind. He stood, used the wrapped-up Iron Sword like a walking staff, and headed for the front door. He was about as discreet as a pink gorilla, and members of the Scourge cut him off.

"No, you donkey skull," Grey Cloak cursed. "What in the Flaming Fence are you doing?"

45

"Where do you think you're going, farmer?" Sash asked Dyphestive. "Can't you see we're having a celebration here?" He stuffed a jug of wine in Dyphestive's chest. "Drink!"

Hemmed in by Sash, Bull, and Hawk, Dyphestive kept his voice down and head low. "I don't want any trouble. I was only going to check on my horse." He showed his hand. "I'm taking her a biscuit."

"Hahaha, a biscuit you say." Sash slapped it out of his hand. "Listen to me. You aren't going anywhere until your pretty friend, Tula, comes back. She owes me a dance."

Dyphestive leaned on his sword like a crutch. "If you say so. But I need to feed my horse." He tried to push by Bull and Hawk, who crowded him. "She gets hungry."

"Look at this sack of meat," Hawk said in cocky voice. "He's as big as Bull." He poked Dyphestive in the chest. "What do they feed you, farm boy? A barrel of oats every day?"

"Seems to me he likes biscuits," Sash said. "Where is your friend, farmer? The pretty one not covered in fleas. You better hope she didn't step out on me. If she did"—he shoved Dyphestive—"you'll be staying in her place. I might even have you dance with Bull. Ha ha."

In a soft voice, Dyphestive said, "Let me go, please. I don't want trouble. I'll come back once I feed my horse."

Hawk erupted in obnoxious laughter. The lean predator of a man said, "This guy is very passionate about his beast." He put his arm over Dyphestive's shoulder. "Perhaps we should let him bring his horse in for a drink. Bwah-ha-ha-ha-hah!"

The Scourge cackled like hyenas.

"Would you like that, big farmer? Huh?" Sash forcefully asked. He stooped over and tried to look at Dyphestive's face. "The big one's shy. He must be real ugly."

"Aye, ugly like Bull. Maybe they're brothers!" Hawk flipped Dyphestive's hat off. "Let's get a closer look at you."

Dyphestive caught his hat before it hit the floor. He tried to cover his face, tucking his chin.

Sash stopped his hand. "Wait a moment." He got closer. "I know you." A dagger appeared in his hand, and he held it before Dyphestive. "Ease back and lower that hat."

On command, he lowered the straw hat and smiled brightly. "Remember me, fellas?"

Bull gave a confused grunt.

"You!" Sash said.

Dyphestive burst into action. He swatted Sash's hand aside in one smooth motion, stuck his hat in Bull's face, and slugged him in the jaw. Bull fell like a tree. Before the Iron Sword hit the floor, Dyphestive snatched it, swung it around his body, and knocked Sash and Hawk onto the floor.

Steel scraped out of a sheath, and footsteps charged his way from behind. The sweet song of metal splitting air crawled in his ears. He blocked the attack on his back with the Iron Sword, pivoted around on his knee, and faced Katrina.

"You're a dead man." Rugged and attractive, the green-haired beauty snaked out another sword and chopped down.

Dyphestive caught the blade in the palm of his hand. Steel sank through flesh and hit bone-like metal. He bent her blade like a spoon and jerked it free of her hand.

"Impossible." She stumbled back into tables and chairs. "No one can do that."

Honzur's hands crackled, and his eyes lit up like fire. Cords of lightning snaked up his arms covered in tattoos that shone like silver. He fired a blast of energy that struck Dyphestive full in the chest and knocked him through the glass window. Dyphestive bounced off the porch and rolled into a trough of water.

Grey Cloak pulled him out of the water by the hair on his head. "How do you feel?"

Dyphestive smiled. "We can take them."

The Scourge poured out of the tavern and into the street—all of them except for Bull, who'd been knocked out cold.

"Well, well, well," Sash said, his sword in hand. The sashes he wore came alive like snakes. "Who do we have here?"

"Your worst nightmare," Grey Cloak commented.

"No, it looks like a couple of Talon's pigeons. Come to steal our dragon charms, eh? A bold move. A fatal move." He looked about. "I hope you knew better than to come alone, because we're going to slaughter you."

Dyphestive stepped out of the trough dripping wet. "It's going to be the other way around." He saw Katrina's fearful eyes. "Ask her. She knows."

Sash gave her a concerned look. "What's he talking about?"

"He bent my sword with his bare hand, and his wound healed. My blow should have severed his hand." She cringed. "He didn't even flinch."

"Where's your backbone, Katrina? We've faced crea-tures far more dangerous than them." Sash stepped forward, sword in hand, with his ribbons poised like snakes to strike. Bull wandered through the tavern door, rubbing his jaw, club in hand. "Time to teach Talon a lesson. Permanently. Scourge, attack!"

Katrina and Squirrel moved in on Grey Cloak. Katrina wielded her longsword and dagger, while Squirrel came at him with a small bullwhip and dagger. She cracked the leather. *Pop!*

"Really?" Grey Cloak asked. "They send the two of you after me? Is it because I'm not as threatening? I'm insulted."

"You still talk too much." Katrina rushed him and sliced at his neck.

Grey Cloak ducked, and the blade whistled overhead. *Swish!*

He blocked Katrina's stab from a dagger, spun into her, and kissed her cheek. "I love your hair. You look fantastic in green braids." He swept her legs out from under her, and she landed flat on her back.

Squirrel's whip cracked at his feet. He danced away. The tip of the whip burst with amber fire with every snap.

"A fine weapon," Grey Cloak teased. "If only you could hit me with it, that would be something."

Squirrel flicked her dagger at him. "Hah!"

The dagger came at him like a buzzing bee.

Grey Cloak plucked the blade out of the air inches from his face. It buzzed in his grasp, stinging his hand. "Ow!" He dropped it.

Crack!

The bullwhip coiled around his neck and sent a painful shock through his extremities, forcing him to his knees. "Aaaargh!"

"We've got him now, Katrina! Finish him!" Squirrel said.

Katrina rose with the sword in her white-knuckled grip. With her jaw clenched, she marched straight toward him and lifted her razor-sharp blade over her head. "Goodbye, Grey Cloak."

Dyphestive faced the three opposing warriors with no fear. He'd faced worse in his short days and stood fully prepared to handle them. He drew forth the Iron Sword—still wrapped in burlap—stuck his chin out, and grinned. "You might want to walk away before you get hurt."

Sash started to dash in for an attack then stopped. "Honzur, now!"

Out of the corner of his eye, Dyphestive caught Honzur standing out of harm's way on the porch, mumbling quickly and twitching his fingers. The dust beneath Dyphestive's feet exploded and coated him in grit from head to toe. Blinded, he coughed and tried to wipe his eyes. The crust on his body hardened, and his limbs became sluggish and slow.

"Take it to him, Bull!" Sash ordered.

Dyphestive saw the musclebound warrior come right at him. He tried to lift his sword to block the club. He was slow, far too slow. The metal end of Bull's club connected with his skull and knocked him flat on the ground.

"Get him, Bull!" Sash ordered. "Break every bone in his body!"

Bull's club went up and came down. He mercilessly hammered Dyphestive. Sash and Hawk joined in, stomping and kicking him with cruel and reckless fury.

Grey Cloak jabbed Katrina in the gut with the Rod of Weapons. The energized jolt he sent into her scale mail shook her all over. She dropped her sword and fell to her hands and knees, spasming.

A charge of fire burned his neck as the whip started to

constrict around his throat. His eyebrows knitted together, and he gave Squirrel a nasty look. "You're going to regret this, you dirty little ferret."

The messy-haired woman grinned. "It looks like you're the only one who's going to regret anything."

With increasing pain spreading through his body, and his air supply cut off, he grabbed the burning bullwhip and jerked it out of Squirrel's fingertips.

She shrieked. "Impossible!"

Grey Cloak uncoiled the whip from his neck. "Nothing's impossible when you're a legend like me."

Squirrel turned to make a run for it.

With a flick of the whip, Grey Cloak caught her around the neck and jerked her off her feet. He reeled her in like a flipping fish and glowered down at her. "How does this feel?" He sent the fires of the Flaming Fence straight into her.

Her body jumped a foot off the ground. She kicked, screamed, wobbled, and passed out.

Katrina crawled toward her sword.

He stepped on it. In a charming voice, he said, "You sided with the wrong mercenaries. A decision you'll soon regret."

She looked up and offered a disheveled smile. "I already do."

"Good." Grey Cloak drove the Rod of Weapons into her

back and shocked her until her body went still. "Life is full of regrets."

Dyphestive took the beating. His pride didn't. The twisted sneers and mocking laughter of his wicked enemies went through him like a hot knife through butter. He'd had enough of evil. Something snapped. He growled.

"Stay down, farm boy! We aren't finished with you yet!" Sash hollered.

Battling against the enchanted sluggishness, Dyphestive crawled to his hands and knees. Hawk and Sash stood on either side of him, kicking him in the gut. Bull clubbed his back. He continued to rise.

"Stay down, you fool!" Sash said.

He puffed for his breath.

Gasp. "You shouldn't be moving. Honzur, what did you do to him? What did you do? Raise the dead? He should be dead."

The Scourge wizard made no reply.

"Fine, I'll finish him myself."

Sash's ribbons jumped off his body and started to bind Dyphestive's arm and legs together.

He stuck his sword into Dyphestive's shoulder. "How's that feel?"

"*Goooooood!*" Dyphestive said dangerously.

Hawk's face paled. He stepped back. "Sash, he ain't dying."

"Oh, he'll die whether his body believes it or not." Sash cocked his sword back and aimed for the heart. "Good night, farm boy!" He thrust.

Dyphestive's limbs suddenly loosened. He ripped through the ribbons and turned his chest away. The blade sliced across his chest.

Sash overstepped.

Dyphestive punched his exposed jaw into tomorrow. *Whop!*

He turned on Bull. Bull brought his club down on Dyphestive's skull. The thick length of wood snapped. Like a dumb ape, Bull stared at the broken end and gave a confused grunt. When he looked back up, he didn't see Dyphestive's fist coming.

Pow!

Hawk dropped his sword and ran away in a cloud of dust.

Grey Cloak strolled over to Dyphestive. He dusted off his hands. "Well, that was easy."

"Yes, it was," Zanna agreed. She stood on the porch, smirking, with Honzur sprawled at her feet.

47

———

NO ONE DIED, and the local authorities hauled the Scourge away to the dungeons, but not before Grey Cloak cleaned them out.

Traveling the dusty roads out of Portham, he rolled three dragon charms in the palm of his hand. "I don't know why we didn't just rob them before. It seemed pretty easy."

"We weren't a match for them before, or at least it was close." Dyphestive rubbed his jaw. "I think my bones are getting harder. Did you see the beating Bull gave me? It didn't hurt any more than a pillow."

"You're blossoming. Both of you," Zanna said.

"Blossoming?" Grey Cloak held Streak in his arms and fed the runt dragon a biscuit. "Care to explain? I don't know that I like the idea of turning into a flower."

Zanna laughed gently. "A natural goes through two

stages. When they are young, their powers reveal themselves during the ripening. They show greater skills than others. If they are properly developed, one can become very strong, and in your case, bond with dragons. But not all do. There are naturals who choose a different way of the world. Like Hercullon or Mad Wolf. However, the two of you were born to ride dragons. That's your calling."

"As for blossoming, well, that's when the full extent of your powers is revealed. It comes through trials and endurance. You're pushed to your limits, and your abilities *blossom*." She took Streak from Grey Cloak. "It's a beautiful thing to see in action. Grey Cloak, when the barbarians swamped you, you let out a pulse of wizardry that could crack stone. Dyphestive, your powers of invulnerability are growing, much like your father's, but I warn you, everyone has a weakness. Don't get cocky."

Dyphestive opened and closed his hand. "Are you saying I can't be hurt?"

"You can be hurt, but not by ordinary means." She patted him on the back. "It's an extraordinary gift."

"Are my abilities extraordinary? I mean, most naturals can do what I do," Grey Cloak said. "I can summon wizardry and use it to charge up weapons. So can they. How come Dyphestive's powers are different?"

"That is the way of the world," she said. "But from what I've seen, you are talented in summoning the wizard fire. The pulses of energy you summon are unique to say the least. Have you used any other powers I haven't seen yet?"

"I don't know." He shrugged. "The cloak offers a lot of them. A couple of times I was able to run really fast. I always figured that was the cloak."

"Interesting." Zanna stopped on the dirt road and took off her shoes. "Race me."

"Race you?" He laughed. "I don't want to embarrass you, Mother."

She set Streak down. "Humor me."

"I want to race." Streak drummed his twin tails on the ground, stirring up the dust. "I bet I'm faster than both of you."

"Fine." He gave her a bored look. "Seeing as we have a decade of seasons to burn, why not?" He swung the cloak off his shoulders and laid the rod on top of it. He pointed. "See where those elm trees start at the end of the road? We'll race to there."

"Are you ready?" she asked.

He nodded.

"Go!" Zanna took off like she was slung from a sling, leaving Grey Cloak in her cloud of dust. By the time the dust cleared, she was waving at him from the elm trees.

His jaw hung.

"That was fast," Dyphestive said. "You aren't that fast. I don't think anyone is."

Zanna walked back. "I'm sorry. Didn't you hear me say go?"

Grey Cloak looked at her feet and took off his boots. "Let's try that again. Dyphestive, this time, you say go."

Dyphestive nodded. "All right. Go."

Zanna dusted him. He didn't make it halfway to the trees before she arrived at the elms.

She jogged back to him. "That's better." She took his hand.

He pulled it away.

"Don't be a sore loser. You need practice." She gave him a head nod. "Run with me."

They took off down the road, half-speed, stride for stride. Zanna picked up the pace. He matched it. The wind started to whistle in his ears.

"Stay with me. Push harder!" she said.

Grey Cloak stretched his long strides to their limits. He picked up speed and started to gain. "I'm doing it!" he shouted. It was like running for the first time. His blood flowed with exhilaration. He'd never run so fast before, aside from the time they'd battled the Scourge long ago. He'd never repeated the action until now. "I'm going to catch you!"

Zanna stretched the lead, and in a few winks of a lash, they covered more ground than he could possibly have imagined. She slowed to a stop.

He caught up, sweating and panting. "How?" He moaned delightfully.

"Superior fleetness is another natural gift that only reveals itself in elves, though not all of us." She fluffed her hair. "Ah, that felt good."

Streak flew into their midst and landed near their feet. "That was fast but not as fast as me. Who wants the next race?"

48

WITH STREAK SCOUTING AHEAD, the trio headed north, following Zanna's lead. They passed through a small town, bought horses and modest travel gear, and rode hard into the night. Even though they didn't need rest, the horses did, so they made camp by the stream.

Dyphestive gathered fallen wood and branches. Streak's hot spit turned the kindling into flame.

Zanna returned from the woods with a small buck slung over her shoulders. With a butcher's precision, she gutted the dead beast, and it wasn't long before they all enjoyed cooked venison. They ate quietly underneath a blanket of clouds that slowly drifted across the sky, revealing bright stars from time to time.

"Thanks for dinner, Zanna." Grey Cloak wiped the juice off his fingers onto a napkin. "Now, if you don't mind, do you care to disclose the secret location where we're traveling?"

She ate a hunk of meat off the tip of her dagger. "Don't you like surprises?"

"I do," Dyphestive said.

Streak returned, dragging a possum in his mouth. He set it down. "So do I." The possum came to life and waddled away in a hurry. "Oh well. This venison smells better."

Zanna continued to eat.

"You're avoiding the question, Zanna. Out with it," Grey Cloak insisted.

"Another Wizard Watch tower lies north of here. It's the best place—"

"Oh no!" Grey Cloak shook his head. "I've had my fill of the towers. We've had our fill of the towers. Every time we go in, we end up somewhere else."

Zanna showed her hands in a sign of submission. "You have to trust me. The towers are the best place to hide. And it's the best way to throw the Scourge from our trail. They'll be hounding us. You know that. We can't allow that to happen."

"They won't catch us."

She stared at him seriously from across the low-burning fire. "What do you think will happen when the Scourge reports to the Riskers they encountered you? Riskers will be combing the hills and climbs of all Westerlund. They'll be relentless. If we're captured now, all will be lost."

Grey Cloak locked his fingers behind his head, looked up, and sighed. He wanted no part of the Wizard Watch. "First, we don't know if the Scourge will pursue us. Second, if I were them, I wouldn't be telling anyone we lost three dragon charms. Would you? And third, we have *three*"—he showed his fingers—"charms, including my fourth. We can handle any Riskers that come our way if need be. As for using the Wizard Watch for sanctuary, heh, I'll take my chances."

Zanna frowned. "You're putting everything at risk. The only fair way to settle this is by putting it to a vote."

He waved his hands. "Hold on. We only vote without a leader, but I'm the leader, and I say we hide somewhere else."

Zanna turned her attention to Dyphestive. "What do you say, Festive? Vote, or follow Dindae?"

"Call me Grey Cloak." He gave his brother a hopeful look. "What do you say?"

With a solemn voice, Dyphestive said, "Forgive me, brother, but I think we should do what your mother says."

Grey Cloak stiffened. "Well, that doesn't change a thing. Streak has a say."

All eyes fell upon the little dragon, whose nose was deep in fresh deer carcass.

Streak lifted his head. "What was that? I wasn't listening."

"Do you think we should go to the Wizard Watch or not?" Zanna asked.

"I go where Grey Cloak goes."

Grey Cloak smirked. "It's a tie."

"That's not a fair vote," Zanna said. "Will you set your pride aside and trust me? I've only helped since I arrived."

"True, but you aren't a wizard." He stood up and held the rod over his shoulders, stretching from side to side. "I've learned my lesson and finally agree with Anya."

"Son, your father, Jerrik, was a wizard. We have allies on the inside we can trust. Please, believe me."

Dyphestive offered him a pleading look. "If we go into the towers, we can move from one territory to another. The Scourge, or Riskers, will never catch us. Right, Zanna?"

"That's the plan. We enter in Westerlund. We exit in any other territory. Our trail will be lost." Zanna cut another hunk of meat, put it on a stick, and hung it over the flames. "It's the best move we can make."

"I can't believe I'm going to go along with this, but fine." He pointed the rod between the two of them. "But if anything squirrely happens, it's on the two of you, not me."

They made it to the northwestern corner of Westerlund, days away from Loose Boot in the north, without any trouble. The air was chill, the terrain rocky, and the horses nickered and whinnied on their trek through the twisting hills.

"Strange place," Grey Cloak commented. "A perfect place for a Wizard Watch."

The white cliffs were porous, the vegetation sparse, making for an odd valley. The wind had a high-pitched whistle when it picked up with haunting effect. The sightings of bright quartz minerals packed in small deposits in the earth began to increase in number. The rocks glowed in an assortment of colors.

Zanna led them through the hills, but it was Streak who flew back and landed on Grey Cloak's head. "I found it. At the top of the hill, you'll see it. Big, tall, lean, like an obelisk. Pretty boring, actually." He spread his wings.

Grey Cloak grabbed his feet. "Stay."

"If you insist." Streak yawned and crawled into the cloak's hood. "I'm tired of flying anyway. Wake me if you meet anyone interesting."

The horses fought their way up the slippery, rocky hills and stopped at the top. They overlooked the valley where the Wizard Watch stood. The ancient stone structure reaching toward the sky stood on a rise in the land. It was surrounded by rings of rock formations creating a crude maze. No visible doors or windows marked the tower, only empty archways on every level, where birds nested.

Grey Cloak shrugged off the chill running down his spine. The towers had been a source of dismay. He had little good to say about them. But with news that his father, Jerrik, was a member of the Wizard Watch, he opened a doorway of trust.

"I know it looks complicated, but I'll lead the way. I've been to this tower more than a few times." Zanna gave her horse a gentle kick, and the beast began its trek downhill. "Come, it won't be long."

Grey Cloak looked at Dyphestive. "We don't have to do this."

"Don't you trust your own mother?" Dyphestive led his horse down the hill.

Grey Cloak followed, mumbling, "Why should I? We hardly know her. But no one listens to me."

The rock formations surrounding the towers began at the bottom of the hill. Like the surrounding land, the rocks were the color of bone and porous, covered in dead ivy, and worn down by wind and rain, but they were sheer in height, standing over ten feet tall in some places.

Zanna disappeared in a switchback only to be sighted again, waiting until the brothers caught up. She tugged her horse's reins, leading them into another gap, and vanished again.

"This is getting old," Grey Cloak muttered. He considered waking Streak to keep watch from the air above, as he'd lost all sense of direction, even though he could still see the top of the tower looming one hundred and fifty feet above. He spotted Zanna again only to watch her trot out of sight. His heart started to beat in his ears. "If this isn't a trap, I'm a bullywug."

He fell behind, allowing Dyphestive to vanish around the next bend. "I've had it." He kicked his horse into a trot and sped around the corner. He tugged the reins. His horse stopped, shook its head, and snorted.

Zanna and Dyphestive were stopped in front of an archway entrance big enough for a giant.

"We've arrived," Zanna said. "Now all we need to do is wait."

Grey Cloak's racing heart started to slow. "And how long will that be? I'd hate for the Scourge to trap us in your ugly little maze."

The stone wall behind the archway started to vanish. In a few moments, the entrance to the tower was clear.

"Not long at all," Dyphestive said cheerfully.

"Make haste. They won't keep it open for long." Zanna took the lead, and the group went inside.

The tower's entrance chamber was the same as the other tower he'd been in. Several more rings of levels could be seen above, each with wall-to-wall archways. In the middle of the chamber was a huge fountain with water cascading from the top. The waters burbled and echoed inside the vast chamber.

The horses nickered and stomped their hooves.

Grey Cloak glanced over his shoulder. The entrance they'd come through had sealed itself with solid stone, leaving them all alone in the cold, dead room. "Now what, Zanna? Do we wait and exit in another territory?"

She dismounted, led her horse to the fountain, and sat down. "Oh, we're going to wait, because no one is going anywhere, not for many, many years."

Grey Cloak sneered. "I knew it. Dyphestive, how could you be so gullible?"

A wizard approached from the shadowy darkness of the adjacent archway. His black-and-white hair was parted evenly in the middle. His half-and-half robes were the same. There was no mistaking the elf coming their way with a silver-handled cane in hand.

Grey Cloak's temper boiled over. The Rod of Weapons' head burst with flame. "Gossamer the betrayer!" He turned on his mother. "How could you do this?"

Zanna looked back at him and shrugged.

49

THE PRESENT – SAFE HAVEN

ANYA STOOD inside Safe Haven's armory on the dais that held the pedestal bearing the Eye of the Sky Riders. Her eyelids were heavy, and she couldn't remember the last time she'd slept. She and Cinder led the other dragons on the long journey back to the unknown sanctuary hidden in the waters of Lake Flugen, from the Wizard Watch in the Wilds.

Zora, Tatiana, Bowbreaker, Reginald the Razor, and Gorva came with her to the only place they could be assured of safety.

Tatiana entered the chamber and joined her on the dais. The elven sorceress was as beautiful an elf as there was: tall, with strong, elegant features, spellbinding eyes, and a flowing brown ponytail that started in a topknot and came down past her shoulders. "Why don't you rest? I can resume the search."

Anya covered her mouth and hid her yawn, but it was obvious. "I can go longer, but you're welcome to join me."

"I want to thank you for bringing us here. Your trust means a lot to me. To all of us," Tatiana said.

"Well, it was either here or inside the Wizard Watch. You know how that goes."

Tatiana tipped her head and drew down an eyebrow. "Agreed. Have you found anything?"

"This might be the vainest search I've ever initiated. The Dragon Helm could be anywhere in Gapoli. It could be in another world, for all we know." Anya combed her fingers through her sun-bleached red hair. "Black Frost could even have it."

"I don't think so. The Dragon Helm went through the same portal Grey Cloak did. He remained in Gapoli." Tatiana placed her hands on the rim of the eye and looked deep into the moving landscapes of Gapoli. "Might I put some effort into it?"

Anya stepped away. "Be my guest, but the eye is built for Sky Riders, not wizards. Don't get your hopes up."

"I understand, but we do share the common ability of wizardry." Tatiana's fingers scrolled through the images inside the pedestal. "This is a fascinating artifact that the Sky Riders have created. Using the spirits of dragons to be the eyes of this marvel is a work of genius. Do you have any idea who created it?"

Anya shook her head.

Using a gentle touch, Tatiana scrolled over Arrowwood and magnified the image by spreading it. "I see the Wizard Watch in the Wilds is under full guard again."

Anya leaned over. "Yes, I've taken a look. It's a full Black Guard regiment and a host of Riskers. They can have the tower, so far as I'm concerned. They've been nothing but a source of trouble."

Nath ambled into the armory's smaller chamber and joined them on the pedestal. His long, stringy hair hung down over his eyes. The flame-colored locks that brightened his hair had all but turned gray. His broad shoulders were stooped, and his limbs were getting bony. The scale-like skin on his arms had begun to flake. The only things in good condition were his white robes with gold patterns that brought out the fire in his eyes.

"Any luck?" he asked in a scratchy voice.

"No." Anya crossed her arms. "And you don't look well."

Nath cleared his throat. "Never in my life did I ever think I'd hear those words. You really know how to hurt a guy."

"Sorry, I didn't mean—"

"It's a jest. I still have thick scales. I can take it." He peered into the Eye of the Sky Riders. "I wouldn't even know where to start looking for the Dragon Helm."

"I'm trying to focus on strong pockets of magic throughout the realm," Tatiana said. She moved the image over all of the Wizard Watch towers spread out across the land. "The towers are the strongest source." She moved the image north. "As is Dark Mountain."

Anya touched the clear glass-like surface in the pedestal and moved the image away. "Don't get too close to Dark Mountain. We can't take the risk that Black Frost and his minions will sense us."

"Of course," Tatiana said flatly. She moved the picture over Monarch City. "I sense strong sources of magic here, but I don't get a sense of the dragon charms. Of course, they won't be that easy to detect, but it would help if we had one in our possession."

"Perhaps I can help." Zora arrived and hopped up to the pedestal. "Or did you forget that I have a Dragon Charm?" The half-elven rogue's full auburn locks were cut below her pointed ears, allowing the tips to show. The charm in her hand was the size of an egg but flat like a stone. It carried a warm pink fire within. She handed it to Tatiana. "Here you go."

Anya frowned at Zora. "Why didn't you give me the charm earlier?"

"I forgot I had it in my possession until I was digging around in here." Zora rummaged through the leather satchel strapped around her chest that Crane had given her. "Besides, you were too busy brooding. I thought I'd better leave you alone."

"This will help." Tatiana gave a quick smile. "This will help greatly."

50

EPILOGUE

"QUICKER! QUICKER!" Inside the subterranean caverns of Safe Haven, Bowbreaker the elf trained with Razor and Gorva. It was man versus orc, fighting with jo sticks, trying to get the best of one another. "You need to be more aggressive, deadly, accurate," Bowbreaker demanded.

Gorva ducked a jab from Razor and swept his legs out from under him with her stick.

He landed flat on his back, jumped up again, and delivered a quick poke in her gut.

She doubled over. "Oof."

"Enough!" Bowbreaker stated. His long, silky hair was as black as ravens' wings. His jaw was hard and his forehead creaseless, and he showed no expression at all. He wore only a pair of buckskin trousers, and his chest and shoulder muscles were well-defined. "That was well done, Razor. You're getting quicker on your feet."

"I'm a lot quicker with steel in hand." Razor's full head of brown hair was as damp as a mop. Beads of sweat rolled down the bare-chested man's muscular back and broad shoulders. "These sticks aren't going to do me any good in a real fight."

"You need balance," Bowbreaker said. "A sword won't always be available."

"And a stick will?" Razor tossed the staff to Bowbreaker. "Hah." He eyed Gorva. The orc woman didn't show a drop of sweat. Her coarse black hair was in braids down past her shoulders. She only wore a top and bottom made out of animals' skins that showed off her athletic figure. "Aren't you even winded?"

"Not in the slightest," she said.

He rolled his eyes. "Sheesh."

Gorva patted her flat belly. "That was a good lick. Well done." She bumped forearms with him. "Your skills are improving."

Razor brushed his hair out of his eyes. "And why wouldn't they be? We've been doing nothing but training for weeks. And for what? To hide in the cave and wait. They don't even have ale down here."

"Agreed. I'm as restless as you." Bowbreaker spun the jo stick around his body. "It's not natural for an elf to live in a cave. I miss the trees, the wind, the song of the leaves."

"Yes, well, I miss the wine, the women, the smell of sweet perfume so strong it will knock you over." He looked at Gorva. "Speaking of perfume, have you ever tried any?"

Gorva returned a flat stare. "One of these days, I'm going to pull your tongue out."

Razor stuck out his tongue. "Wouldn't you like to try?"

"Still at it, I see." Nath crept up on them from out of nowhere. He coughed dryly. "I remember those days, but now they seem so far away."

"No disrespect meant, but you don't look so well, old man," Razor said.

Even stooped over, Nath still stood taller than Razor. He peered into Razor's eyes. "Live over a thousand years and see how well you look. Regardless, my time is short. Come, everyone, Anya and Tatiana have found something."

"Finally, we might see some action," Razor said.

They joined Anya, Zora, and Tatiana inside the Eye of the Sky Riders chamber. The three women wore grave expressions.

"What's wrong, ladies?" Razor asked in his charming manner. "You look like someone died."

Tatiana held a Dragon Charm in her hand that twinkled like a pink star. She stood behind the pedestal. "We found the Helm."

Razor brightened. "That's a good thing, right?"

None of the women standing on the pedestal said a word.

"What's the problem?" He scratched his head. "Somebody say something."

Anya motioned for the others to come up on the dais. "Come and look."

The inside of the pedestal looked like a bowl of flames. It was so realistic that Razor swore he could feel the heat from it. "What in the world is that?"

Tatiana clasped her hands in front of her mouth, and with a dire look, she said, "That is the Flaming Fence. The Dragon Helm lies in the Nether Realm, the land where nothing living can survive."

Will Talon cross the Flaming Fence and retrieve the Dragon Helm?

How will Grey Cloak and Dyphestive escape the tower now that Zanna Paydark double-crossed them?

Grab Book 15 Now! The Devil's Snare and find out all of the answers and more! Click here!

And please leave a Review on Barbarian Backlash. They are a huge help. LINK.

Learn more about Fogle Boon, the shrewd wizard summons from the Figurine of Heroes, in the International bestselling series, The Darkslayer Omnibus.

And if you haven't already, signup for my newsletter and grab 3 FREE books including the Dragon Wars Prequel.
WWW.DRAGONWARSBOOKS.COM

Teachers and Students, if you would like to order paperback copies for you library or classroom, email craig@thedarkslayer.com to receive a special discount.

Gear up in this Dragon Wars body armor enchanted with a +2 Coolness factor/+4 at Gaming Conventions. Sizes range from halfling (Small) to Ogre (XXL). LINK . www.society6.com

ABOUT THE AUTHOR

Please leave a review. They are a huge help to me! Post a review, email me the link, and I'll send you a free copy of Book Two. Here is a link.

*Check me out on Bookbub and follow: HalloranOn-BookBub.

*I'd love it if you would subscribe to my mailing list: www.craighalloran.com.

*On Facebook, you can find me at The Darkslayer Report or Craig Halloran.

*Twitter, Twitter, Twitter. I am there too: www.twitter.com/CraigHalloran.

*And of course, you can always email me at craig@thedarkslayer.com.

See my book lists below!

OTHER BOOKS

Craig Halloran resides with his family outside his hometown of Charleston, West Virginia. When he isn't entertaining mankind, he is seeking adventure, working out, or watching sports. To learn more about him, go to www.thedarkslayer.com.

Check out all my great stories...

Free Books

> **The Red Citadel and the Sorcerer's Power**
> The Darkslayer: Brutal Beginnings
> Nath Dragon—Quest for the Thunderstone

The Chronicles of Dragon Series 1 (10-book series)

> The Hero, the Sword and the Dragons (Book 1)

Dragon Bones and Tombstones (Book 2)

Terror at the Temple (Book 3)

Clutch of the Cleric (Book 4)

Hunt for the Hero (Book 5)

Siege at the Settlements (Book 6)

Strife in the Sky (Book 7)

Fight and the Fury (Book 8)

War in the Winds (Book 9)

Finale (Book 10)

Boxset 1-5

Boxset 6-10

Collector's Edition 1-10

Tail of the Dragon, The Chronicles of Dragon, Series 2 (10-book series)

Tail of the Dragon #1

Claws of the Dragon #2

Battle of the Dragon #3

Eyes of the Dragon #4

Flight of the Dragon #5

Trial of the Dragon #6

Judgement of the Dragon #7

Wrath of the Dragon #8

Power of the Dragon #9

Hour of the Dragon #10

Boxset 1-5

Boxset 6-10

Collector's Edition 1-10

The Odyssey of Nath Dragon Series (New Series) (Prequel to Chronicles of Dragon)

Exiled

Enslaved

Deadly

Hunted

Strife

The Darkslayer Series 1 (6-book series)

Wrath of the Royals (Book 1)

Blades in the Night (Book 2)

Underling Revenge (Book 3)

Danger and the Druid (Book 4)

Outrage in the Outlands (Book 5)

Chaos at the Castle (Book 6)

Boxset 1-3

Boxset 4-6

Omnibus 1-6

The Darkslayer: Bish and Bone, Series 2 (10-book series)

Bish and Bone (Book 1)

Black Blood (Book 2)

Red Death (Book 3)

Lethal Liaisons (Book 4)

Torment and Terror (Book 5)

Brigands and Badlands (Book 6)

War in the Wasteland (Book 7)

Slaughter in the Streets (Book 8)

Hunt of the Beast (Book 9)

The Battle for Bone (Book 10)

Boxset 1-5

Boxset 6-10

Bish and Bone Omnibus (Books 1-10)

CLASH OF HEROES: Nath Dragon meets The Darkslayer mini series

Book 1

Book 2

Book 3

The Henchmen Chronicles

The King's Henchmen

The King's Assassin

The King's Prisoner

The King's Conjurer

The King's Enemies

The King's Spies

The Gamma Earth Cycle

Escape from the Dominion

Flight from the Dominion

Prison of the Dominion

The Supernatural Bounty Hunter Files (10-book series)

Smoke Rising: Book 1

I Smell Smoke: Book 2

Where There's Smoke: Book 3

Smoke on the Water: Book 4

Smoke and Mirrors: Book 5

Up in Smoke: Book 6

Smoke Signals: Book 7

Holy Smoke: Book 8

Smoke Happens: Book 9

Smoke Out: Book 10

Boxset 1-5

Boxset 6-10

Collector's Edition 1-10

Zombie Impact Series

Zombie Day Care: Book 1

Zombie Rehab: Book 2

Zombie Warfare: Book 3

Boxset: Books 1-3

OTHER WORKS & NOVELLAS

The Red Citadel and the Sorcerer's Power